Second language acquisition of English reflexives by Taiwanese speakers of Mandarin Chinese

馬 修
Guy Matthews

封面設計：實踐大學教務處出版組

University of Essex

Department of
Language and Linguistics
Fax: 01206 872198

From Professor Roger Hawkins
e-mail: roghawk@essex.ac.uk
direct dial: +44 1206 872235

Colchester Campus
Wivenhoe Park
Colchester CO4 3SQ
United Kingdom
Telephone: 01206 873333
Fax: 01206 873598
Web: www.essex.ac.uk

8th June 2009

To whom it may concern

Dr Guy Matthews
PhD, University of Essex

I certify that the award of Doctor of Philosophy was conferred on Guy Matthews by
the University of Essex on 22nd May 2008. This is the highest academic award for
original research that it is possible to achieve in the United Kingdom.

The title of Dr Matthews' PhD thesis is "Second language acquisition of English
reflexives by Taiwanese speakers of Mandarin Chinese". This work used the way that
speakers of Mandarin Chinese interpret reflexive pronouns both in Mandarin and
English in order to address a number of general theoretical issues in the study of
second language acquisition. The work is an important contribution to the field, and is
of very high quality, as confirmed by the external examiner, Dr Heather Marsden
(University of York), and the internal examiner, Professor Louisa Sadler.

Yours faithfully,

[signature]

Department of Language
and Linguistics
University of Essex
Colchester
Essex CO4 3SQ
Great Britain

Professor Roger Hawkins
PhD thesis supervisor

• Acknowledgements •

This research would have been impossible to complete without the help of others. The biggest debt of gratitude must be to Roger Hawkins. His insightful comments and criticisms clarified my thinking about certain areas. Therefore, the finished work has undoubtedly been greatly improved as a result.

I must also thank the native speakers of Taiwanese and Mandarin who helped me. Without the help of Yu-ching (Margaret) Chang, Shi-jen (Jennifer) Chen, Shin-ping (Brian) Liu and Ya-wen (Joy) Kuo it would have been impossible to construct the Taiwanese and Mandarin tests. In addition, their patience in answering my questions on native-speaker intuitions on a variety of sentences is gratefully appreciated.

Thanks should also go to Dr. Jeff Salyer for providing a source of academic and research advice. In addition, his perspective on the English test sentences was very informative and useful.

I am also grateful to the Mandarin, Taiwanese and English-speaking informants who volunteered their time in taking the tests.

On a personal note I would like to thank Margaret Chang, and Margaret and Michael Matthews for their support.

Finally, though the help of others was vital any mistakes or errors are entirely my own.

Second language acquisition of English reflexives
by Taiwanese speakers of Mandarin Chinese

· Abstract ·

This research is principally concerned with the question of whether, and to what extent, the second language acquisition (SLA) of reflexives can be explained in terms of access to innate language universals. It assumes that Universal Grammar (UG) is a fundamental part of first language acquisition and is, therefore, within the generative framework

A critical analysis of the theoretical status of UG in SLA is combined with an examination of syntactic models of binding that have been developed following Chomsky's (1981) Binding Theory. Following Cole and others, the theory of head movement at LF is proposed as a syntactic basis to explain binding, as it is argued it meets both typological and theoretical criteria of adequacy. However, it is also argued that this, or any other syntactic theory, is not capable of providing a complete explanation for the behaviour of reflexives. Therefore, semantic accounts of binding are analysed. In particular, theories associated with the notion of logophoricity are advanced. The subsequent analysis of previous research and the empirical testing, conducted in both first (L1) and second language (L2), are based on the assumption of an integrated model of head movement at LF and logophoricity.

This study describes the testing of Mandarin speakers in both their L1 and L2 (English). This methodology is designed to ensure that a clear picture of the learners' knowledge of reflexives is obtained. Thus, any conclusions are based upon a comprehensive understanding of their L1 grammar and their ILG (inter-language grammar).

Thus, the aim of this research is to provide insights as to whether a combined syntactic and semantic model of binding can account for L1 and L2 grammars.

· Contents ·

• Chapter 1 •

Theoretical Considerations in Studying Second Language Acquisition

1.1 Introduction

This study is concerned with the question of whether the linguistic behaviour of non-native speakers can be accounted for in terms of an underlying Universal Grammar (UG). The particular area of L2 knowledge that is investigated in relation to this issue, in the present study, is the acquisition of reflexive binding properties in English by native speakers of Mandarin Chinese from Taiwan. It makes the assumption that native speakers' linguistic competence can be understood in terms of the availability of the universal linguistic principles and language variable parameters of UG (Chomsky 1976, 1981, 1995). Thus, a child acquiring an L1 attains an unconscious, principled linguistic system, or grammar, which allows that child to know what is, and what is not, admissible in the language. Following Chomsky (1959) Atkinson (1992), Pinker (1994) and others the native speaker is able to do this because there is an innate, biological basis to language acquisition that is available to all human beings. Only in the case of extreme mental or circumstantial abnormalities[1] is the utilization of this innate ability prevented.

1

This language faculty is held to be species specific and not synonymous with intelligence. Arguments in support of this view can be made on the grounds that the success and the order and pattern of language acquisition is relatively uniform. In addition, acquisition is rapid and effortless in that no special instruction or teaching is needed. Thus, a child acquiring an L1 starts with an initial zero state S_o, where he or she has an innate UG language endowment but no language specific knowledge. Linguistic input interacts with UG and the child moves through a succession of mental representations or grammars (G_1, G_2 .... G_n). Finally, the individual will reach a steady state with a mature adult grammar L1 S_s. This is represented schematically in figure 1.1 (adapted from White 2003: 3, Fig. 1.1).

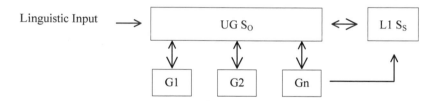

Figure 1.1 Model of Acquisition of L1 Grammar

1.2 Language acquisition in L1 and L2

Chomsky (1976:13) argues that "Every 'theory of learning' even worth considering incorporates an innateness hypothesis". However, there is a possibility that non-linguistic innate faculties are the basis of language acquisition. As White (2003) notes:

> *it is conceivable that an innate capacity for language acquisition could be general rather than domain specific and*

> *that cognitive principles not unique to language learning might be implicated.* (2003:4)

However, any theory needs to account for the fact that children seem to have a greater knowledge of the subtle and abstract properties of their L1 than can be accounted for by the linguistic input. This discrepancy between the input and knowledge is known as the "logical problem of language acquisition" or the problem of "poverty-of-the-stimulus."

A fundamental question is whether the same poverty-of-the-stimulus arguments also apply with L2 acquisition. If L2 learners also have knowledge of features of the language that could not have been induced from the linguistic input, then this would be evidence that UG also constrains IL grammars. However, for this evidence to be convincing it is necessary to show that such knowledge did not come from explicit explanation and correction, or from learning principles, that are not linguistic-specific, or from the L1.

There are several reasons why it is not so easy to assume that the same process applies in the acquisition of an L2 Grammar or interlanguage grammar. Though Corder (1967), Selinker (1972) and Adjemian (1976) have argued that L2 learners' grammar is systematic and governed by rules it is not clear that these rules are necessarily based on UG. As Coppieters (1987) comments:

> *It is possible to argue that the same process of setting principles and parameters applies in SLA, but this is open to dispute on a number of grounds. It is apparent that L2 learning is comparatively unsuccessful. It does not share the same uniform and inexorable nature of L1 acquisition. It can be claimed that L2 learners never attain totally native level intuitions.* (1987: 553)

The differences between L1 and L2 acquisition mentioned above could be ascribed to fundamental differences between the L1 and L2 learners.

Firstly, the L2 learner is, by definition, older than the L1 learner. If more than one language is simultaneously acquired, it would seem to be totally arbitrary and, therefore, meaningless to label them as the L1, L2 etc. In addition to the relative general cognitive and developmental maturity of L2 learners, the Critical Period Hypothesis of Lenneberg (1967) posits that entirely successful language acquisition is only possible for pre-pubescent learners, as only they can make use of an innate "language acquisition device." Therefore, the argument is that language acquisition is a biologically predetermined, maturational process.2 If this is true, then post-pubescent L2 learners might have no, or limited, access to innate linguistic capabilities. As there is the possibility of dispute about whether a language acquired by a pre-pubescent learner is an L1 or an L2, L2 learners will be defined as post-pubescent and adult learners.

The second fundamental difference is that the L2 learner has an existing grammar, i.e. the L1 grammar. The L1 learner has an initial state where, though the innate language faculty exists, there are no language specified principles or parameters. The L2 learner, however, already has the actual parameters and principles of an L1 instantiated. Thus, there is a question of whether UG still exists as an "independent faculty" outside its instantiation in the L1. Thus, as White (2003:59) points out, "the question of whether UG becomes a particular grammar or remains distinct from particular grammars is central." As Cook and Newson (1996:125) argue, "[w]ith different starting points to first and second language acquisition it is hardly surprising that the end result is different."

1.3 Access to UG in SLA

There are conflicting theories and ideas about whether, and to what extent, L2 learners have access to UG. Though different researchers have categorized these theories in different ways, using different terminology, they can be somewhat simplified by being regarded as four main hypotheses. The first hypothesis is that UG is unavailable in SLA. This carries the implication, for researchers accepting a generative framework for L1 acquisition, that L1 and L2 acquisition are fundamentally different processes. The second hypothesis is that L1 and L2 acquisition are fundamentally analogous, with UG being completely available. However, a third hypothesis is that though UG is available, there is a difference between L1 and L2 acquisition because the L2 learner's initial state is not the zero state S_o. This means that although the learner has access to all principles and parameters even if they are not instantiated in the L1 or if the L1 settings are different, the interlanguage (henceforth ILG) of an L2 learner can vary from that of a native speaker. The final hypothesis is that it is possible learners have partial access to UG; perhaps being only able to access those areas of UG instantiated in the L1.

1.3.1 No access to UG

There are certain implications if one argues that the learner has access no access to UG. First, it seems necessary to postulate an alternative strategy to account for L2 acquisition. This is because there appear to be strong poverty-of-the-stimulus arguments regarding the discrepancy between linguistic input and the knowledge of the L2 learner. Sharwood Smith (1989) argues that in second language research:

> *however rich the communicative context of utterances addressed to the language learner and however helpful the native speakers are or teachers may be, there are subtle and complex features of human language that cannot be provided*

> *by the usual kind of input nor even by the usual type of*
> *correction and explanation.* (1989:14)

Therefore, a possible model would be that the L2 learner would proceed through a series of IL grammars ILG_1, ILG_2... ILG_n. Thus, the learner will potentially arrive at a steady state IL grammar ILG S_s. This is shown in Figure 1.2 (drawing on White 2003: 59, Fig. 3.1). Though this seems analogous to the L1 process a crucial difference is that UG is unavailable. This has the implication that grammars are constructed using other non-linguistic faculties of the mind. This leads to the possibility of wild or rogue IL grammars which diverge from linguistic theory in that the constraints of UG, which preclude such grammars in an L1, are not applicable.

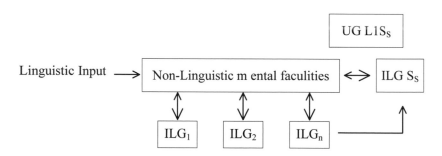

Figure 1.2 Model of L2 Acquisition with No Access to UG

Clahsen and Muysken (1986) analyzed the acquisition of word order in German by both L1 and L2 learners. Citing, among others, Clahsen's (1982) longitudinal study of the L1 acquisition of the underlying subject-object-verb (SOV) order, they posit that this can be analyzed as a four stage process, which can be explained by the nature of the input and the constraints of UG. However, citing data from Clahsen, Meisel and Pienemann (1983), who collected both cross-sectional and longitudinal data from Spanish, Portugese and Italian speakers, and

Dittmar (1981), who collected data from Turkish speakers, they propose that non-native speakers of German follow a six-step developmental sequence in acquiring the SOV order. Clahsen and Muysken argue that this order is explicable in terms of syntactic movement and generalizations which occur with non-natural syntactic categories. Thus, L1 speakers will place finite verbs in the sentence-final position when they start to use embedded clauses in sentences like:

> **(1) Guck was ich in mein tasche   hab.**
> **Look what I   in my   pocket have.**
> **"Look what I have in my pocket." (Clahsen and Muysken 1986: 99)**

However, both speakers of Romance (= SVO) languages and Turkish (= SOV) predominantly use SVO structures. Verb-final structures in the ILGs of German learners tend to occur in SV or OSV structures such as the following example from a Turkish speaker:

> **(2) Meine bruder er helfen.**
> **My brother he help;**
> **"He helps my brother." (Clahsen and Muysken 1986: 108)**

This it is argued is because their verb final sentences are not base-generated, but are derived from an SVO order with a complement-preposing rule.

> **(3) Ich will nicht heiraten, weil diese jungen sind nicht nett.**
> **I want not marry because these boys are not neat.**
> **"I don't want to marry because these boys aren't neat"**
> **(Clahsen and Muysken 1986:109)**

Therfore sentence (3), which was used by a Turkish speaker, demonstrates an SVO order and is grammatically similar to sentences produced by the Romance speakers.

This leads them to conclude that, "L2 learners are not only creating a rule system which is far more complicated than their native system, but also which is not definable in linguistic theory" (1986:116).

Therefore, if UG is unavailable we would expect to find grammars which are "not definable in linguistic theory" or "wild." However, Du Plessis, Solin, Travis and White (1987) and Schwartz and Tomaselli (1990) challenged the non-natural word order rules of Clahsen and Muysken. Though their respective analyses of the IL stages of L2 learners are not identical they both posit that the learners are operating with IL grammars which are consistent with the constraints of UG.

Bley-Vroman (1989) posits the Fundamental Difference Hypothesis and claims that L1 and L2 learning are intrinsically very different. His argument is that L2 learning is not characterized by the uniformity of success found in L1 acquisition as the learner often reaches a ceiling and no further progress is made (i.e. fossilization). This means that the L2 learner very rarely attains a native level of knowledge of the L2. In addition, he notes variation between different L2 individuals in their L2 acquisition. Such factors as teaching methodologies, learner strategies, learner correction and affective factors like motivation seem to be important in L2 acquisition. This contrasts with the highly uniform and inexorable nature of L1 acquisition. Thus, Bley-Vroman's conclusion is that L2 learning is more akin to non-linguistic problem solving than it is to L1 acquisition operating within the constraints of UG.

Cook (1993) argues that UG is only applicable to core grammar. Hence, the apparent lack of success of many L2 learners does not provide convincing evidence in support of the hypothesis that UG is unavailable in L2 acquisition. Cook notes that: "UG does not encompass all, or even most, of L2 learning." and that "The lack of completeness or of success has nothing to do with the UG model unless L2 knowledge is less complete in the core areas covered by UG" (1993:212). Thus, following this line of argument it would seem that the fact that L2 learners do not seem to reach the level of attainment of L1 speakers is not per se an indication of the unavailability to them of UG.

A criticism of accounts which maintain the non-availability of UG in L2 acquisition is that they are underdeveloped and lack explicitness (White, 1989 and Schwartz, 1991). The greater explicitness of UG-based accounts entails that they are more powerful in that they offer more explicit predictions which are testable. The explicit predictions arising from UG-based accounts will be discussed in this chapter. Furthermore, UG-based accounts of binding, and the testing based on such accounts, will be discussed in chapters 2 and 3. Researchers such as Flynn (1983), Newmeyer and Weinberger (1988) and Thomas (1993) have argued that a factor in favour of research based on UG is its explanatory power. Thomas (1993) notes that:

> *without specific proposals as to what general abilities or strategies are entailed in adult L2 learning, it is impossible to determine how they could be applied to the intricate task of language learning.* (1993:15)

If UG is not involved in L2 acquisition it would seem to be necessary to posit an account which can show exactly how subtle linguistic behaviour is acquired. Such an account would then be a testable alternative.

1.3.2 Full access to UG

If L2 learners have full access to UG it would seem that an assumption could be made that those learners would be able to arrive at final ILGs which are indistinguishable from the S_s grammars of native speakers. Therefore, the acquisition process would be basically the same as in the L1, with linguistic input triggering the setting of principles and parameters, until the final steady state grammar of the L2 learner (IL S_s) is indistinguishable from the steady state grammar of a native speaker. Thus any language errors would be either due to performance factors or simply due to the fact that there had been insufficient input to allow instantiation of the correct settings in the language. Thus we have the following model 1.3 (adapted from White 2003: 61, Fig 3.2):

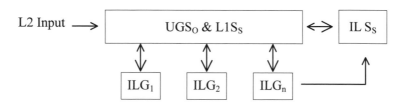

Figure 1.3 Model of L2 Acquisition with Full Access to UG

However, this model makes the assumption that the initial state S_o is basically the same for the L2 learner as it is for the L1 learner, and that the L1 grammar does not influence, interfere with, or act as an obstacle in L2 acquisition. Evidence to support this hypothesis would be the fact that L2 learners successfully incorporate a facet of UG not present in their L1, as this would obviate the possibility that they are merely transferring their L1 setting into the L2, or not directly using

UG, but basing their IL grammar on some ad hoc non-linguistic problem solving, where that grammar is based on an analogy with the features of their L1. In a pioneering study Ritchie (1978) examined the Right Roof Constraint proposed by Ross (1967) and Chomsky (1973). He claimed that his Japanese subjects did not allow movement out of an embedded clause. Since Ritchie argues that Japanese has no right movement their knowledge of the constraint could not have come from their L1. This would seem to offer support for what Cook and Newson (1996:291) describe as "direct access", where "L2 learners start from scratch; they have direct access to UG and are uninfluenced by the L1" and White (2000:135) calls No Transfer/ Full Access, where "the L1 final state does not constitute the L2 learner's grammar or mental representation at any stage."

However, Hawkins (2001) commenting on full access theories notes that there is a practical limitation on this access in that if the learner has not been exposed to enough examples to establish relevant principles or parameters they will initially use L1 principles:

> *the learner has had insufficient time to experience enough samples of L2 data to establish the relevant categories. And it is this which gives rise to the transfer of syntactic properties from the L1. In the absence of relevant experience of the L2, the learner relies on the syntax of the L1 to construct sentences.* (2001: 71)

Nevertheless, if the basic validity of this model is accepted the learner once having being exposed to sufficient input, will move to new UG-sanctioned settings for the L2. Therefore, the input interacts directly with UG and consequently the model of acquisition can basically be seen as the same as in LI acquisition. Thus, the L2 and L1 learners' initial states and their respective intermediate grammars are similar. This means that as far as the acquisition of an L2 is concerned,

UG is unchanged by the fact that there is already an instantiation of a language. Consequently, all principles and parameters whether they are instantiated in the L1 or not, are available in the L2.   Epstein, Flynn and Martohardjono (1996, 1998) advocate the Strong Continuity Hypothesis, where they argue that "at all stages of acquisition L2 learners have knowledge of the full inventory of both lexical and functional syntactic categories provided by Universal Grammar" (1998:61).

However, others have argued that though the L2 learner has full access to all the principles and parameters of UG the way the L2 input interacts with UG is not the same. In L1 acquisition innate language knowledge is at a zero state So; there is no language specific knowledge. This contrasts with the situation in L2 acquisition where the initial state is Si. In this case the L2 learner will initially transfer principles and parameters from the L1. However, as they still have full access to UG these can be reset. This model is shown in Figure 1.4. Schwartz and Sprouse's (1996) Full Transfer/ Full Access model takes the initial L2 grammar as the L1 Ss in its entirety. Thus, the learner has full access to UG at all times, and if the L2 input conflicts with their ILG then that learner is able to use UG to reset their ILG. Therefore, the learner is able to accommodate features, functional categories and parameters that are not found in the L1 into ILGs that are constrained by UG. However, there is a clear contrast in the ILGs of learners between the "No Transfer/ Full Access' model and the "Full Transfer/ Full Access' model.

1.3.3 Differences in Initial States

However other researchers have taken a different approach suggesting that L2 learners do not start with a UG representation based on the L1 in its entirety. Therefore, in the model depicted in figure 1.4 (again, drawing on White 2003: 61, Fig. 6.3) S_i is not synonymous with the final steady state grammar of a native speaker (L1 S_s). One such proposal is The Minimal Tree Hypothesis[3] of Vainikka and Young-Scholten (1994, 1996a, 1996b). In this hypothesis functional categories are taken to be entirely absent from the initial grammar of L2 learners. The learner will take lexical categories and their properties from their L1. They can then be subsequently modified when and if sufficient L2 input necessitates it. However, functional categories and their projections are at no stage transferred from the L1. This means, as UG is still available, they emerge gradually with exposure to the L2 input. Thus, although the final steady state grammar of the L2 learner (IL S_s) may be indistinguishable from that of a native speaker of a particular language there will be variation between the grammars of children acquiring it as an L1 and those who learn it as an L2.

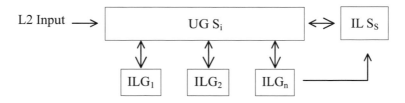

Figure 1.4 Model of L2 Acquisition with access to UG,
where the L1 impacts upon the ILGs of the second language learner

An illustration of empirical evidence supporting L1 transfer (whether the transfer is partial or full is not clear) and subsequent acquisition of L2 settings in a domain that will be of central interest in the present study (reflexive binding) comes from Yuan's (1998) study of Japanese- and English-native-speaking learners of Mandarin. In this study Japanese-intermediate learners' judgments of the acceptability of long-distance antecedents for the reflexive ziji did not differ significantly from those of the native-speaking controls. Reflexives which can be bound long-distance are found in Japanese. Thus, these results would be consistent with both L1 transfer or with the successful acquisition of the L2 setting. However, the English-intermediate learners were much less likely to accept long-distance antecedents. As such binding is not present in English this can be seen as evidence of the effects of the L1. However, the advanced group of English speakers showed a greater acceptance of long-distance antecedents. This it can be argued shows that they are successfully acquiring the L2 settings.

1.3.4 Partial access to UG

The fourth hypothesis is that although UG is available, access to it is impaired or restricted in L2 acquisition. In what Cook (1988:182) terms the "indirect access" hypothesis the L2 learner only has access to those aspects of UG that are present in the L1. Thus, L2 learners will have available any principles which are universal to human languages, as universal principles will be present in the L1; they will also be able to incorporate into their L2 grammars any parameters instantiated in the L1. However, they are unable to realize any new setting and as White (1990:127) comments UG is, "dead as an active force in L2 acquisition". Thus, we have a model where the grammar initially incorporates extant principles and perhaps parameters of UG, but UG is

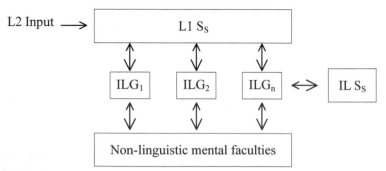

Figure 1.5 Model of L2 Acquisition with Access restricted to extant UG

unavailable so that L2 input fails to trigger new parameter settings. This is shown schematically in figure 1.5 (expanding upon White 2003: 90, Fig. 3.3). However researchers have given differing interpretations on whether this would mean the IL grammars of native speakers are UG constained.

It is possible that if the L2 input is in conflict with the mental-grammatical representation learners will construct grammars which are not describable in linguistic theory. As Thomas (1993) comments L2 learners:

> *cannot rely on knowledge of UG to construct a grammar of L2 which differs parametrically from that of the L1. As a result.... grammars will not be constrained by UG in cases where L1 and L2 parameter settings diverge.* (1993:16)

Thus, the learner encountering input inconsistent with the parameter setting of his or her L1 would have to resort to non-linguistic problem solving in constructing a grammar. Clahsen and Hong (1995) argue for the unavailability of parameter settings. Their position is that though the learner has access to UG principles instantiated in the L1, properties that in the L1 are dependent on a particular parameter setting are not in such a relationship in the L2. In their study of Korean speakers acquiring German they argue that in L1 German acquisition the elimination of null subjects from the child's grammar is a feature which co-varies with the acquisition of agreement. However, only a minority of the Korean speakers showed a similar co-variance leading to Clahsen and Hong's analysis of a breakdown in parameter setting in an L2.

Other researchers have maintained that despite the breakdown in the ability to reset parameters IL grammars can still be constrained by UG. Tsimpli and Roussou (1991) claim parameters associated with functional features are inaccessible to L2 learners. Supported by evidence from their study of Greek speakers, they argue that the cluster of properties associated with the pro-drop parameter do not occur in L2 acquisition. The apparent success that learners demonstrate is ascribed to the construction of a different grammar than that of native English speakers. This "different grammar" is still held to be constrained by the principles of UG.[4] Hawkins and Chan (1997) argue for the unavailability of functional features not found in the L1. They argue that as Cantonese lacks the [wh] feature Cantonese speakers learning English do not derive relative clauses by operator movement in sentences like:

> **(4) The girl who I like is here. (Hawkins and Chan, 1997: 190)**

Following Huang (1984) when resumptive pronouns are null in Chinese the empty category is held to be pro. The Cantonese speakers generate wh-phrases in Spec CP, which are then bound to a null resumptive pro. This analysis means that the ILGs of the Cantonese speakers are based on the L1 and are consistent with UG.

1.4 Theory and Empirical Research

Though, as discussed in the preceding sections, there has been considerable debate as to the place of UG in SLA it is necessary to be careful in constructing and interpreting empirical data as supporting a particular theoretical framework.

Evidence of differences between acquisition of a language as an L2 and as an L1 cannot be taken as prima facie evidence of lack of access to UG because of real differences between L1 and L2 acquisition. Thus, as Hawkins (2001:345) comments, "contextual differences inevitably give rise to differences in the course of development of L2 grammars." Such differences could be a result of such factors as the differences in age, cognitive development, presence of a language, affective factors leading to fossilization and the nature of the input they receive. Thus, it is a fallacy to argue that if the judgments of an L2 learner diverge from those of a native speaker, this shows that UG is not operating in the L2. In addition, it is not sufficient to construct a non-UG analysis of the data. As Schwartz and Sprouse (2000) comment:

> *This cannot be done merely by constructing an analysis of an Interlanguage data set in such a way that the analysis is "UG-incompatible" on the adoption of some particular theory of UG. One can always concoct a UG-incompatible analysis of data ....To not locate a UG-compatible analysis of the data may simply show lack of imagination, since there may be a UG-compatible analysis of the data after all.* (2000: 157)

They argue that it is necessary to also show that "L2 acquisition is not undetermined by the input". Though, these points are reasonable it does leave the researcher in an invidious position in that it is unclear how one would prove this negative proposition. However, despite various attempts (for example, Clahsen and Muysken 1986, Newmeyer 1998) it seems that a non-UG-constrained IL grammar has yet to be unambiguously described.

It would seem that the most parsimonious explanation of an L2 learner whose linguistic insights into a language are indistinguishable from those of a native speaker is that he or she has a UG-constrained grammar. However, if an analysis of the IL grammar leads to a UG-constrained analysis it would seem necessary to also show that poverty-of-the-stimulus arguments are present. Thus, clear evidence that learners are demonstrating behaviour that is consistent with UG, but could not be determined by the input and cannot be explained in terms of L1 transfer is powerful evidence in support of the hypothesis that UG plays a role in L2 acquisition. However, if the evidence points to a divergence between the grammars of L1 and L2 acquirers, the researcher is faced with a variety of different possible interpretations. Thus, such evidence could show that the learner is operating in accordance with the models outlined in section 1.3.3 or possibly that access in the L2 is only partial, as outlined in section 1.3.4

This study will examine reflexive binding in English by native speakers of Taiwanese and Mandarin Chinese. It will investigate whether the responses of informants throw any light onto the questions discussed in this chapter, i.e. the place of UG in SLA. The methodology employed will be to outline a theoretical model of binding and then to investigate the intuitions of informants with respect to reflexive binding in both the L1 and the L2. Thus, any conclusions drawn will be empirically supported.

The organization of the rest of the thesis is as follows. In chapter 2 theoretical models of binding will be discussed and a "working model" will be adopted. Chapter 3 considers previous studies of the SLA of reflexives to see what they can tell us about the issues raised in the first two chapters. Chapter 4 looks into the factors that were relevant to the design of the tests used in this study and discusses pilot tests that were conducted in Taiwanese and Mandarin. Chapter 5 describes and reports the results of tests on reflexive binding in Mandarin. In chapter 6, the same informants are then tested on reflexive binding in English. Chapter 7 presents a theoretical framework which seems to account for the data from both Mandarin and English. The final chapter will summarize how the findings from the empirical studies stand in relation to:

(i)   The models of L1 acquisition outlined in chapter 1
(ii) Previous studies of the SLA of reflexives
(iii) The mixed semantic and syntactic model discussed in chapter 7.

Notes

1. See Curtis (1977) for a discussion of "Genie" where extreme circumstantial abnormalities are a possible cause of an inability to fully acquire language.
2. See Pinker (1994).
3. Various researchers (Clahsen 1990/1991, Vainikka 1993/4, Clahsen, Eisenbeiss and Vainikka 1994)) have proposed that children lack a full complement of functional categories in their L1.
4. However, see Liceras (1997) for an argument that the inability to reset parameters leads to the possibility of ad hoc solutions.

Second language acquisition of English reflexives
by Taiwanese speakers of Mandarin Chinese

• Chapter 2 •

Theories on the Binding of Reflexives

2.1 Introduction

This study is concerned with the second language acquisition of reflexives. Therefore, this chapter will outline theoretical models that are designed to account for binding, with a view to arriving at a set of linguistic assumptions that will form the basis for investigation of acquisition. The first part will discuss syntactic theories, concentrating on accounts based on head-to-head movement. The second part will look at non-syntactic accounts, concentrating on logophoricity. As this study is concerned with Mandarin, special attention will be directed towards explaining long-distance binding.

2.2 Binding theory

Binding theory is concerned with looking at the distribution of NPs having the same reference. Reinhart (1983) noted that NPs within a sentence can manifest three logical possibilities with respect to coreference. Coreference with another NP can be (i) obligatory, (ii) optional, or (iii) proscribed. The following pair of sentences, both containing three NPs, demonstrates these three possibilities.

(1) **Ann$_i$ told Betty$_j$ to wash herself$_{*i/j/*k}$**

(2) **Ann$_i$ told Betty$_j$ to wash her$_{i/*j/k}$**

Sentence 1 shows obligatory coreference between the second and third NPs but coreference between the first and third is proscribed. This contrasts with sentence 2, where coreference is optional (but not obligatory) between the first and third NPs, but proscribed between the second and third.

A starting point for describing the behaviour of anaphors and pronominals within the generative tradition is Lectures on Government and Binding (Chomsky 1981). In LGB NPs are classified into four types based on two abstract features: [anaphor] and [pronominal]. The four types of NPs are shown in (3) with their respective abstract features.

(3) **Typology of NPs**

	Overt	Empty
[+anaphor, -pronominal]	lexical anaphor	NP-trace
[-anaphor, +pronominal]	pronominal	pro
[+anaphor, +pronominal]	—	PRO
[-anaphor, -pronominal]	R-expression	wh-trace

The NPs are subject to principles A, B and C of binding theory:[1]

(4) **Binding Principles**

Principle A: An anaphor is bound in its governing category.

Principle B: A pronominal is free in its governing category.

Principle C: An R-expression is free.

Chomsky's (1981) definition of the binding domain is:

(5) Binding domain
β binds α iff.
β c-commands α, and β and   α are coindexed.

C-command can be defined as:

(6) c-command
α c-commands β iff α does not dominate β and the first
branching node dominating α also dominates β.

Finally, the local domain is usually defined in terms of a governing category:

(7) Governing category
γ is a governing category for α iff.
γ is the minimal category that contains α and a governor
for α and has a subject.

Examining sentences (1) and (2) again in light of these we find that they account for the referential properties of the NPs. However, though the definition of binding presented in (3) – (7) seems to work for English[2] this does not seem to necessarily be the case with all languages. In particular it was noted early in the literature that long-distance (LD) reflexives occurred in a range of languages.[3] For example, if we examine the Chinese sentence:

(8) Zhangshan$_i$ renwei Xu$_k$ xihuan ziji$_{i/j/k}$.
Zhangshan know Xu like self.
"Zhangshan knows Xu   likes himself."

We see binding of the reflexive, out of the local domain, to the matrix subject, Zhangshan.

Thus, it would seem that the formulation of Binding we have so far fails to account for the data when a variety of languages are studied. This has meant that various researchers have tried to offer theoretical analyses which are better able to incorporate the linguistic evidence. Within the generative framework, a number of proposals have been put forward. Section 2.2 and 2.3 will briefly outline two of the theories that have generated research into the SLA of reflexives.

2.3 Parametric Variation

An early approach was the proposal that what constitutes a binding domain is subject to parametric variation (Manzini and Wexler 1987; Wexler and Manzini, 1987). In this analysis the Governing Category Parameter (GCP) for anaphors has five settings:

> (9) **Governing category parameter**
> γ **is a governing category for α iff, γ is the minimal category that contains α and a governor for α and has**
> **a. a subject; or**
> **b. an Infl; or**
> **c. a Tense; or**
> **d. a "referential" Tense; or**
> **e. a "root" Tense.**

Manzini and Wexler's model also outlined a specific model of learnability: the subset principle. This entailed, for the case of anaphors, that setting a. was the most restrictive setting and also the marked value and learners/ acquirers would initially select that setting, as the different settings are held to be in a hierarchical subset relationship. This relationship can be shown as:

(10) $L(a) \subset L(b) \subset L(c) \subset L(d) \subset L(e)$

This means that if the language in question was at another setting then evidence from primary linguistic data would allow the possibility of resetting of the parameter moving from a more to less restrictive setting.

In addition, Manzini and Wexler postulated the Proper Antecedent Parameter (PAP):

(11) Proper antecedent parameter
A proper antecedent for α is
a. a subject β; or
b. any element β.

Again, the subset principle applies:

(12) $L(a) \subset L(b)$

Within this model, the Lexical Parameterization Hypothesis states that individual lexical items select values of the GCP and PAP. If we take pronominals and anaphors from English, it seems that the setting is consistently (a) for the GCP and (b) for the PAP. However, this uniformity for a setting within a particular language is not mandated by the theory. Thus, in Icelandic Wexler and Manzini posit that different lexical items are associated with three different values: (a), (c) and (d)[4] of the GCP.

However, this model has been criticized, both from a theoretical standpoint, and for its adequacy in accounting for the data from empirical studies of first and second language acquisition. Safir noted that Manzini and Wexler's theory, from being, "crafted with the avoidance of overgeneralization" in mind, runs the risk of being, "confronted with a potential undergeneralization problem" (1987:80). This has led some (Kang, 1988) to criticize the conceptual basis of this analysis, as the fact that the parameters can be set at different values in the same language seems to be at variance with standard generative ideas that languages select from a limited range of parametric options. Thus, as parameters are linked to individual lexical items, the theory can be held to lose explanatory power. In addition, a similar criticism can be made about the existence of the separate GCP and PAP. As Pica (1987) and others have noted, long distance reflexives appear to take subject antecedents. Thus the linguistic data would seem to suggest some connection between less restrictive settings of GCP and the most restrictive PAP setting of (a). Hermon (1992) commented that it is not possible to unify or connect these parameters.[5]

Furthermore, an additional problem with the explanatory power of this model is based on two other typological features of LD reflexives noted in the literature. Firstly, Pica (1984) and Yang (1983) noted that long distance reflexives are monomorphemic, X^0 elements. For example, Hyams and Sigurjónsdóttir (1990), in their analysis of Icelandic, contrast the long distance monomorphemic reflexive sig with the polymorphemic, X^{max} reflexive sjalfan sig. In their analysis sjalfan sig is locally bound, but the morphologically simplex form of the reflexive can be bound long distance. Wexler and Manzini's theory fails to offer any explanatory framework for the difference between simplex and complex reflexives. Furthermore, as was first noted by Huang (1984), LD reflexives can be subject to blocking. Thus in the following sentences:

(13) **Zhangshan$_i$ renwei ni$_j$ xihuan ziji$_{*i/j}$.**
Zhangshan think you like self
"Zhangshan thinks you like him/ yourself."

(14) **Zhangshan$_i$ renwei Lisi$_j$ xihuan ziji$_{i/j}$.**
Zhangshan think Lisi like self.
"Zhangshan thinks you like himself."

The subject of the matrix clause, Zhangshan is not acceptable as the antecedent for the reflexive if intervening potential antecedent has conflicting features.

2.4 Relativized SUBJECT approach

An alternative syntactic approach to explaining reflexives was the relativized SUBJECT[6] framework of Progovac (1992, 1993). Following Pica (1984, 1987) reflexives are classified as a morphologically simplex head, X^o or as a morphologically complex phrasal, X^{max}. Potential antecedents or SUBJECTS for reflexives are relativized in that a SUBJECT for an X^o reflexive is an X^o category only, i.e. Agr. However, X^{max} reflexives must be bound within the domain of a phrasal subject (i.e. NP,IP and NP,NP). This means that SUBJECTS for X^{max} reflexives will be within the same clause as they are X^{max} specifiers. Thus, polymorphemic reflexives are locally bound. Following the analysis of Borer (1989), Agr can be anaphoric or referential; the former being morphologically null, whereas the latter is morphologically overt. If Agr is morphologically overt then the reflexive is bound locally. If Agr is anaphoric and therefore morphologically null then an X^o reflexive can be bound long distance as it can be bound in the domain of a higher Agr.

This analysis leads to the conclusions that (i) monomorphemic reflexives will be capable of being bound by X^o subjects in languages that either do not have overt morphological Agr or do not have it in the structure in question; (ii) that long-distance X^o subjects are possible antecedents, but only if Agr is morphologically null and coindexed with higher Agrs to form an Agr chain; (iii) an Agr chain can only be formed if the Agrs have the same φ-features. If φ-features of an intermediate Agr differ from those of the reflexive, then binding to it and any higher Agrs will be blocked.

2.5 Movement at LF

A third theory in the generative framework was head-to-head movement.[7] Batistella (1989) posited that LD reflexives involve head movement from Infl to Infl at LF. In this analysis developed by Cole and his associates (Cole, Hermon and Sung 1990, Cole and Sung 1994, Cole and Wang 1996) long-distance binding of monomorphemic reflexives is explained in that X^o reflexives can move into a higher X^o position. Therefore, long distance reflexives can be viewed as "only seemingly LD: in all analysis in this group the relationship between the reflexive and its antecedent is covertly local in nature" (Cole and Sung 1994: 356). This movement is shown in figure 2.1 for the canonical sentence:

> **(15) Zhangshan$_i$ renwei Lisi$_j$ zhidao Xu$_k$ xihuan ziji$_{i/j/k}$**
> **Zhangshan think Lisi know Xu like self.**
> **"Zhangshan thinks Lisi knows Xu likes himself."**

Thus, the reflexive ziji first moves from the object position of IP_3 first to V_3 and then is adjoined to I_3 (For the purpose of exposition only movement to Infl and C is shown in Figure 2.1). It is argued that VP is L- marked[8] by the adjunction of the reflexive and is consequently not a barrier. It can then move to C_3 as IP_3 is not a barrier. Movement is then possible to V_2 as again there is no barrier because CP_3 is L-marked.

Thus movement is then syntactically allowed to continue in the same way from V_2 to I_2 and so on until it eventually moves to I_1. Thus, movement is potentially unbounded in this analysis.

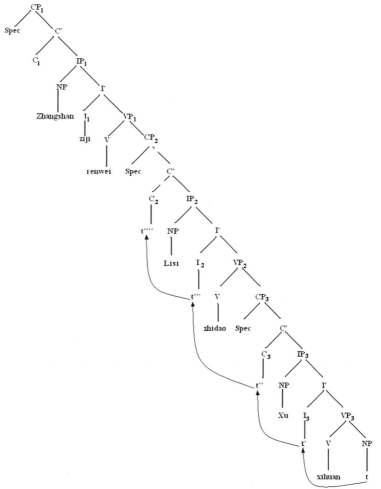

Figure 2.1 Movement at LF
(adapted from Cole and Sung 1994:388-389)

Proponents of this model have pointed out that one of its strengths is that it meets the needs of explanatory adequacy. It provides a framework that accounts for the main typological features of LD reflexives that have been recorded in the literature, namely their morphological simplicity, subject orientation and the blocking effect. The following sections will look at these features with respect to this analysis.

2.5.1 Morphological Simplicity

As was noted by Yang (1983), Pica (1984,1987) and many other writers LD reflexives are typically monomorphemic. This contrasts with polymorphemic reflexives, which are held to be local. Thus, in English, polymorphemic reflexives are local. If we look at an English sentence comparable to (14) we find this to be the case:

(16) John$_i$ thinks Frank$_j$ knows Bill$_k$ likes himself $_{*i/*j/k}$

However, many writers (Huang 1984, Cole Hermon and Sung 1990, Huang and Liu 2001) hold that if the polymorphemic reflexive taziji replaces ziji in sentence 15 then only the local antecedent, Xu is possible.

(17) Zhangshan$_i$ renwei Lisi$_j$ zhidao Xu$_k$ xihuan taziji$_{*i/*j/k}$
Zhangshan think Lisi   know Xu like himself.
"Zhangshan thinks Lisi knows Xu   likes himself."

This contrast between simple and complex reflexives has been noted in a wide variety of other languages, including Icelandic (Hyams and Sigurjonsdottir, 1990), Hindi-Urdu (Davison, 1999) and Italian

(Giorgi,1984). The following Italian examples are from Giorgi (1984: 323-4).

(18) Credo che Mario$_i$ sostenga che tu abbia parlao di se$_i$
      Believe that Mario claimsthat you have spoken of self
      e della sua famiglia in TV.
      and of the his family on TV.
      "I believe that Mario claims you have spoken about him
      and his family on TV."

(19) Gianni$_i$ amasolo se stresso$_i$.
      Gianni loves only himself.

(20) Gianni$_i$ pensa che tuami se stresso$_{*i}$.
      Gianni thinks that you love him self.

The morphological simplicity of LD reflexives is predicted in this theory as reflexives that are heads (X^o) raise into I (the node that dominates them) by head-to-head movement and can be interpreted there. However, morphologically complex reflexives (X^{max}) are maximal projections and adjoin to the immediate phrase where they are interpreted.

2.5.2 Subject Orientation

Pica (1987) observed that LD reflexives are limited to antecedents that are subjects. Evidence for this has also been noted in a variety of languages. For example the reflexive ziji in Mandarin:

(21) Zhangshan$_i$ songgei Lisi$_j$ yizhangziji$_{i/*j}$ dexiangpian.
      Zhangshan give Lisi one CL self DE picture

"**Zhangshan gives Lisi a picture of himself.**" (**Pollard and Xue 2001: 318**)

If we look at the Italian possessive reflexive we see that if it has a LD antecedent it must be a subject.

(22) **Gianni$_i$ ha convinto Osvaldo$_j$ del fatto che la propria$_{i/*j}$ casa**
Gianni has convinced Osvaldo of the fact that the self house
e la piu bella del paese.
is the most beautiful of the village.
"**Gianni has convinced Osvaldo that his own house is the most beautiful in the village.**" (**Giorgi 1984: 331**)

Again, this is a predicted feature of the head-to-head movement account. As X^o reflexives raise to I non-subjects will not c-command the reflexive at LF. Thus, only subjects can be antecedents.

2.5.3 The Blocking Effect

The blocking effect was first noted in Mandarin (Tang, 1989: Huang 1984) and it has principally been discussed in the literature on Chinese and some other East Asian Languages (Huang and Tang 1991; Pan, 2001). The blocking effect precludes higher subjects from being the antecedent if a lower subject differs in person features from that subject. This is shown in figure 2.2 for the sentence:

(23) **Zhangshan$_i$ renwei ni$_j$ zhidao Xu$_k$ xihuan ziji$_{*i/*j/k}$.**
Zhangshan think you know Xu like self.
"**Zhangshan thinks you know Xu likes himself.**"

32

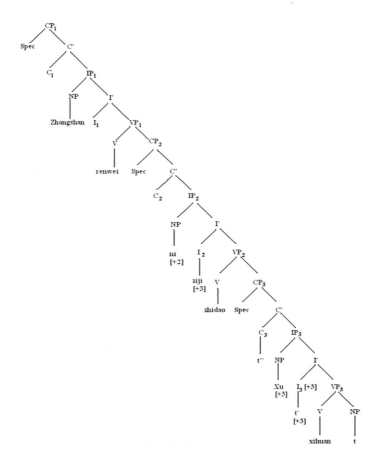

Figure 2.2 The Blocking Effect

Thus, in this example (see figure 2.2) the reflexive adjoins to I as I has no base-generated φ-features, the feature [+3] can percolate up to I_3. As the φ- features [+3] of Spec IP_3 do not conflict, Spec IP_3 is a possible antecedent for the reflexive. However, the φ-features of I_2 [+3] are percolated up. Now when checking the φ-features of Spec IP_2 [+2] a difference is observed. This means that Spec IP_2 is ungrammatical as an antecedent for the reflexive. The intermediate subject is blocked as it differs in person features from the lower subject. In addition as movement is from head-to-head, movement to the matrix subject is also blocked despite the fact that there is no difference in the person features between it and the lowest subject. This follows from the Head Movement Constraint which requires movement to a lower I before movement to a higher one. The reflexive must agree with the φ- features of both the lower and higher Spec positions. Consequently the φ- features of the two Spec's must agree. This effect, it is argued, occurs in languages in which I lacks person features. However, if I is marked for person no blocking occurs. Thus, in Icelandic:

(24) **Olaf$_i$ telur að mér finnist bokin sig$_i$ goð.**
Olaf believes that me-DAT seems-SUB book self good.
"Olaf believes that I consider his book good." (Maling, 1984: 229)

This is explained by percolation of features in the Feature Percolation Principle (FPP)

(25) **The FPP**
a. The features of the mother node and the features of the daughter nodes will be identical.
b. If the features of the daughter nodes conflict, the mother node will have the features of the head node.

Thus, in sentence (23) the conflicting features of the daughter nodes (i.e. 1st and 3rd person) mean that the mother node will take the features of the head node. Therfore, Olaf is the antecedent for the reflexive sig.

2.5.4 Criticisms of the LF head-movement account

Although the LF head-movement account has been influential, a number of criticisms and problems have emerged. The first issue has been the claim that X^{max} reflexives can be involved in LD binding. For example, Pan (1998) and Huang (2000) note that the Mandarin reflexive taziji is not exclusively bound to local antecedents.

> **(26) Xiaoming$_i$ shuo leisheng ba taziji$_i$ xiao le yi tiao.**
>
> **Xiaomingsay thunder BA himself frighten PERF one CL.**
>
> **"Xiaoming said that the loud clash of thunder had given himself a fright." (Huang, 2000: 96)**

However, as Tang (1989) and others have pointed out there is ambiguity between treating taziji as a reflexive or a pronoun ta followed by an emphatic use of the reflexive. The Mandarin examples would not seem to be decisive evidence that X^{max} reflexives can have LD antecedents.

The LD binding of polymorphemic reflexives has also been reported in a range of other languages such as Turkish, (Kornfilt, 1997), English (Kuno, 1987; Zribi-Hertz 1989; Pollard and Sag, 1992; Baker, 1995)

> **(27) But Rupert$_i$ was not unduly worried about Peter's opinion of himself$_j$. (Zribi-Hertz 1989: 709)**

Thus, it seems that at least in some situations it would be impossible to maintain that LD binding of X^{max} reflexives is always prohibited. Thus some researchers have concluded that, "the correlation between locality and X^o-X^{max} status of reflexives is at best a tendency cross-linguistically" (Huang, 2000: 117).

The universality of subject orientation has also been called into question in the literature with several authors providing counter-examples (Xu, 1994; Cole and Wang, 1996; Anagnostopolou and Everaert, 1999).

> **(28) Zhangshan$_i$ yiwei Lisi$_j$ hui ba ni$_k$ dai hui ziji$_{i/j/k}$ de jia.**
> **Zhangshan think Lisi will BA you take back self DE home.**
> **"Zhangshan thought Lisi would take you back to his home." (Cole and Wang, 1996:361)**

In this example we see that the preverbal object is a possible antecedent for the reflexive. However, following the analysis of Cole, Hermon and Huang (2001) ba is taken to be a functional head and the "object" of ba is in the specifier position of the maximal projection which is the complement of ba. The reflexive adjoins to the head of the complement. Thus, c-command requirements would be met allowing both subjects and the NP immediately following ba to be antecedents for the reflexive.

Huang (1994, 2000) comments that the LF head-movement analysis seems unable to account for certain situations where the subcommand condition applies (Tang 1989).

> **(29) The subcommand condition**
> **β subcommands α if and only if β is contained in an NP that c-commands α or that subcommands α, and any argument containing β is in subject position.**

This appears to account for the situation where the subject noun is contained within an NP which is not a potential antecedent due to its inanimacy.

(30) **Zhangshan$_i$ de taidu shi ziji$_i$ bu hao.**

   Zhangshan$_i$ POSS attitude is self not good.

   "Zhangsan's attitude towards himself isn't good"

Thus, in sentence (29) the NP Zhangsan de taidu is inanimate, but is an argument in the subject position. Therefore, the argument contains the animate Zhangshan which can be the antecedent for the reflexive.

However, Huang argues that pragmatic or semantic factors can lead to a relaxation of the FPP.

(31) **Xiaoming$_i$ de fuqin$_j$ de turan qushi$_k$ dui ziji$_{i/??j/*k}$ daji.**

   Xiaoming POSS father POSS sudden death to self strike a blow hen zhong very heavily.

   "Xiaoming's father's sudden death struck a heavy blow on self." (Huang, 2000: 120)

(32) **Xiaozhang$_i$ qing wo$_j$ zuo zai ziji$_{i/*j}$ de shenbian.**

   Xiaozhang ask me sit at self GEN side.

   "Xiaozhang asks me to sit beside self." (Huang, 2000:121)

Thus, in sentence (30) though the head of the NP is inanimate the features of the noun fuqin are percolated up thus making this NP the antecedent for the reflexive. In sentence (31), despite the conflicting φ-features, the higher subject is the (only) acceptable antecedent.

Finally, if we turn to blocking we find that several researchers have pointed out that the LF head-movement account runs into a number of problems. The first problem is that there is evidence that direct objects and obliques, which are not potential binders, can induce blocking:

(33) **Zhangshan$_i$ zhidao Lisi$_j$ gaosu-guo ni$_k$ youguan ziji$_{*i/j/*k}$ degongzuo.**

Zhangshan know Lisi tell-GUO you about self DE work.
"Zhangshan knew that Lisi told you about his work."

(34) Zhangshan$_i$ renwei Lisi$_j$ cong wo$_k$ nar tingshuo-le
ziji$_{*i/j/*k}$.
Zhangshan think Lisi from I there hear-say-PERF self
de fenshu DE score.
"Zhangshan thinks Lisi heard from me his score." (Xue,
Pollard and Sag, 1994)

As the LF head-movement account posits that only c-commanding and
subcommanding subjects induce blocking, sentences such as (32) and
(33) are a challenge.

Furthermore, the presence of various asymmetries in blocking
also poses a challenge to this theory. It has been noted by many
researchers (Tang 1989, Huang and Tang 1991) that there is a number
asymmetry. This would not be a problem if we follow Battistella (1989)
and Cole and Sung (1994) in claiming that number is not an agreement
feature in certain languages such as Chinese. However if we look at the
following sentences this does not seem to apply.

(35) Xiaolan$_i$ zhidao tamen$_j$ kanbuqi ziji$_{i/j}$.
Xiaolan know they look down on self.
"Xiaolan knows they look down on him."

(36) Tamen$_i$ zhidao Xiaolan$_j$ kanbuqi ziji$_{*i/j}$.
They know Xiaolan look down on self.
"They know Xiaolan looks down on them." (Huang,
2000: 121)

It has also been repeatedly noted that there is an asymmetry between
first and second person and third person pronouns. This means that a

first or second person intermediate subject will prevent the reflexive from taking a higher third person antecedent. However, this does not appear to be the case when the situation is reversed and a third person subject is in a "blocking position". This can be seen in the following examples.

(37) **Zhangsan$_i$ zhidao wo/ni$_j$ xihuan ziji$_{*i/j}$.**
Zhangsan know I/you like self.
"Zhangsan knows I/you like myself/yourself."

(38) **Wo/ni$_i$ zhidao Zhangsan$_j$ xihuan ziji$_{i/j}$.[9]**
I/ you know Zhangsan likes self.
"I/ you know Zhangsan likes my/your/himself."

This would seem to directly contradict the analysis of sentence (22) (repeated here as (38)):

(39) **Zhangshan$_i$ renwei ni$_j$ zhidao Xu$_k$ xihuan ziji$_{*i/*j/k}$.**
Zhangshan think you know Xu like self.
"Zhangshan thinks you know Xu likes himself."

This contradiction seems to arise from the fact that different native speakers do not seem to share the same intuitions and/ or judgments as to the acceptability of certain antecedents in such cases.[10]

This asymmetry also has been reported as extending to cases where the pronoun is in a non-subject position and hence not a potential antecedent. Li (1993: 163) gives the following examples:

(40) **Baoyu$_i$ yiwei wo$_j$ dexuesheng$_k$ bu xihuan ziji$_{*i/*j/k}$.**
Baoyu think I DE student not like self.
"Baoyu thinks my student does not like himself."

(41) Baoyu$_i$ yiwei Lisi$_j$ de xuesheng$_k$ bu xihuan ziji$_{*i/*j/k}$.
Baoyu think Lisi DE student not like self.
"Baoyu thinks Lisi's student does not like him/ himself."

2.5.5 Conclusion

There is a considerable amount of evidence to suggest that the LF head-movement analysis provides a framework which seems to account for most of the data. In addition, this model allows researchers to make firm predictions. However, it also seems that there is sufficient evidence that an exclusively syntactic approach is incapable of accounting for all the counter-examples that have emerged. Thus, it is necessary to augment the analysis offered so far with a semantic component. The most promising area seems to be examining the possibility that logophoricity can further explain the behaviour of anaphora.

2.6 Alternative Accounts of Binding

In contrast to the syntactic theories outlined in this chapter so far a number of authors have concentrated on explanations of LD binding which are semantically or pragmatically oriented. Chen (1992) offered a functional account in which discourse properties explain the distribution of the reflexive. Xu (1993, 1994) gave an explanation based on thematic prominence. Huang's (1997) account is based on neo-Gricean pragmatic principles. Part of the motivation for research into non-syntactic explanations arises from the examples of variation among languages in how pragmatic and or discourse factors influence the distribution of LD reflexives. Perhaps some of the most promising non-syntactic areas of research have been based on the idea of logophoricity (Hagège, 1974) and de se (Chiercha, 1989). Therefore, the following section will examine these areas.

2.6.1 Logophoricity

The term "logophoric pronoun" refers to a group of pronouns first described in certain African languages (Hagège, 1974; Clements 1975). Logophoricity can be defined as:

> *The "perspective" of an internal protagonist of a sentence or discourse, as opposed to that of the current, external speaker, is being reported by some morphological and/ or syntactic means* . (Huang 2000: 172)

It follows that pronoun usage depends upon factors such as the "internal protagonist's' words, thoughts, knowledge and perception. Thus, logophoric pronouns are oriented towards certain types of antecedents. For example in Ewe:

(42) **Kofi$_i$ be e$_{*1}$ –dzo.**
Kofi$_i$ say heleft
"Kofi said that he left."

(43) **Kofi$_i$ be me$_{*1}$ –dzo.**
Kofi$_i$ say I left.
"Kofi said that I left."

(44) **Kofi$_i$ be ye$_1$ –dzo.**
Kofi$_i$ say LOG left.
"Kofi said that he/I left." (Sells, 1987: 448)

The pronoun e refers to a non-speaker and non-addressee while me refers to the speaker. However the logophoric pronoun ye can only refer to the subject of the verb. It cannot refer to any other person.

Frajzyngier (1993:174-5) examined Mupun and catalogued three distinct classes of pronouns.[11]

(45) Wu$_1$ sat nə di$_1$ ta dee n-jos.
He say COMP he stop stay PREP-Jos.
"He said that he should stay in Jos."

(46) Wu$_1$ sat nə wu$_2$ ta dee n jos.
He say COMP he stop stay PREP-Jos.
"He said that he should stay in Jos".

(47) N-sat n-wur$_1$ nə gwar$_1$ ji.
I-say PREP-he COMP he come.
"I told him that he should come."

(48) N-sat n-wur$_1$ nə wur$_2$ ji.
I-sayPREP-he COMP he come.
"I told him that he should come."

As can be seen from the above examples (where the subscript numbers show coreference) the logophoric pronoun di in sentence (44) shows coreference with the matrix subject. However, the use of the alternative pronoun wu in sentence (45) indicates that there is no coreference. A similar situation arises in the coreference possibilities between sentences (46) and (47) when the logophoric addressee pronoun gwar is contrasted with the pronoun wur.

2.6.2 Logophoricity and LD reflexives.

Many researchers have used the ideas of logophoricity in accounting for LD reflexives. Kuno (1987) argues that when the choice of whether to use a pronoun or a reflexive is not determined syntactically the choice is based on point of view. Hellan's (1991) analysis of Norwegian and Icelandic sees binding relationships in term of reflexives being bound if they fall within the scope or perspective of the antecedent. Sells (1987) posited that logophoricity was not a unified notion and produced a taxonomical classification of logophoric requirements into three types: SOURCE, SELF and PIVOT in the Discourse Representation Theory (DRT). In this theory SOURCE refers to the source of communication, SELF refers to the mental state or attitude of the proposition that the sentence describes and PIVOT is the deictic or perspective centre. Thus a logophor refers to an individual whose (a) speech or thought, (b) state of consciousness, or (c) point of view is being reported. This individual may be internal (a protagonist in the sentence) or external (the speaker) to the sentence.

Sells argues that a logophorically acceptable antecedent for a LD reflexive must be one of these three types. However, the requirements vary between languages. For example, in Icelandic he claims that antecedents must represent the mental state of the described individual (i.e. SELF), whereas in Japanese the requirement is one of perspective (i.e. PIVOT).[12]

Some researchers have argued that as either SOURCE or SELF are logophoric requirements it may be possible to unify them as a single condition. Chierchia (1989) adopted Lewis's (1979) distinction between de re and de se beliefs. In this analysis, sentences that involve self-ascription (de se) are semantically different from those that do not. Thus, de re requirements represent a relation between a believer and a proposition, whereas with de se reading a relation between a believer and a property is represented.   Consider the following sentence:

> **(49) Pavarotti crede che I propri/ suoi pantaloni siano in fiamme.**
>
> **Pavarotti believes that the self/his pants are in flame.**
>
> **"Pavarotti believes that his pants are on fire."**

In this sentence both the reflexive propri and the pronoun suoi produce well formed sentences. Compare the English equivalent sentence:

> **(50) Pavarotti believes that his pants are on fire.**

Chierchia argues that there is an ambiguity in both the English and the Italian sentence (with the pronoun suoi) when they are bound by the subject, Pavarotti. The ambiguity lies in the fact that Pavarotti may or may not be aware that it is in fact his own pants that are on fire. The speaker of the sentence is aware that Pavarotti and his/ suoi refer to the same person. However this is not necessarily the case with Pavarotti. If, for example, Pavarotti sees a singer from behind on a TV monitor he may believe that the singer's pants are on fire, but he may not realize that that singer is in fact himself. In either case he can be said to have a de re belief in the truth of the proposition. However, only when Pavarotti self-ascribes the property of the pants being on fire is there a de se reading. In such a case the use of the reflexive propri is appropriate as in Italian it is only possible when de se requirements are met.This division is captured in the representation in (50).

> **(51) a.(λx (believe (x,x's pants are on fire))) (P)**   **de re**
>
> **b. believe (P, λx (x's pants are on fire))**   **de se**

Thus, if we look at the following sentence:

(52) Lisi$_i$ zhidao Xu xihuan ziji$_i$.
    Lisi know Xu like self.
    "Lisi$_i$ knows Xu likes him$_i$"

This sentence under the head-movement account detailed in section 2.4 would have the following syntactic representation when the reflexive is LD.

(53) Lisi [ziji$_i$ zhidao [Xu xihuan t$_i$]].

If we compare sentence (52) with the semantic representation following Chierchia'sanalysis we would get:

(54) zhidao (Lisi, λx (Xu xihaun x))

Again following Chierchia, a corresponding syntactic structure would seem to be:

(55) Lisi zhidao [$_{IP}$ ziji$_i$-O [Xu xihuan t$_i$]][13]

Given this analysis, it would seem that the syntactic representation in sentence (52) does not match the representation in sentence (54).

    This would seem to show a difference between the structure proposed by Chierchia and those of the LF head-movement analysis, as the LD reflexive is in the CP of the complement clause in LF rather than the I or AGR of the matrix clause. Cole, Hermon and Lee (2001) propose that ziji moves to a pre-VP position so the matrix clause does not c-command the reflexive. This would produce the following syntactic representation:

(56) Lisi [$_{VP}$ ziji$_i$-O [zhidao [t'$_i$ [Xu xihuan t$_i$]]]]

As Cole, Hermon and Lee (2001) note, these two structures would entail different predictions as to whether post-verbal objects would be potential antecedents. Following the analysis of sentence (54) both matrix subjects and objects should be acceptable antecedents. However, according to (55) post-verbal objects would not be potential antecedents. They give examples from Teochew to support the claim that post-verbal objects cannot be the antecedent for reflexive kaki.[14]

> (57) **Sengseh$_i$ ga hakseng$_j$ kaki $_{i/*j}$ zornimue siosim.**
> **Teacher teach student self how careful.**
> **"The teacher$_i$ teaches students how he should be careful." (Cole et al., 2001: 21)**

2.6.3 Evidence for Logophoricity in Chinese

Several researchers have looked at long distance binding in Chinese in terms of logophoricity. Yu (1992) noted that it is possible to have the reflexive ziji in a sentence which does not contain a possible antecedent. In such cases ziji refers to the speaker and can be seen as representing "I", "me" or "myself". As such the SOURCE is the external speaker. This clearly means that ziji is capable of occurring in contexts where it is not syntactically bound. Huang and Liu (2001: 160) discuss various examples of the use of ziji:

> (58) **Yinwei Lisi piping ziji$_i$, suoyi Zhangsan$_i$ hen shengqi.**
> **Because Lisi criticize self so Zhangsan very angry.**
> **"Because Lisi criticized him, Zhangsan was very angry."**

> (59) **(Dang) Lisi piping ziji$_i$ de shihou, Zhangsan$_i$ zheng zai kan shu.**

(at) Lisi criticize self DE moment Zhangsan$_i$ right at read book.

"At the moment Lisi was criticizing him, Zhangsan was reading."

(60) Zhangsan$_i$ shuo (dang) Lisi piping ziji$_i$ de shihou, ta zheng zai.

Zhangsan say (at) Lisi criticize self DE moment he right at kan shu read book.

"Zhangsan said that at the moment Lisi was criticizing him, he was reading."

Huang and Liu noted that the contrast in acceptability of the non-commanding NP, Zhangsan as the antecedent for ziji between sentence (57) and (58). In both sentences Lisi can be seen as the source of the communication. However, Zhangsan is a more acceptable antecedent for ziji in sentence (57) because of the causal relationship between the two clauses. Hence, the strong implication is that Zhangsan is aware of the criticism. Thus, the mental state or attitude of Zhangsan meets the SELF requirement. This contrasts with sentence (58) where the lack of a causal relationship and the implication that Zhangsan might be unaware of the criticism makes LD binding of ziji much less felicitous.   Huang and Liu comment that:

> the status of (sentence (58) ranges from acceptable to somewhat marginal. It seems that this is possible when the speaker, rather than maintaining a neutral perspective, empathizes with the internal protagonist Zhangsan, i.e., taking Zhangsan as the Pivot antecedent of ziji. If the speaker maintains a completely neutral perspective, (sentence (58)) is unacceptable. (Huang and Liu 2001: 160)

Finally, if we consider sentence (59) we find that Zhangsan is now acceptable as the antecedent. This is because Zhangsan is now the (internal) SOURCE.

Following from the preceding analysis, it seems clear that non-syntactic criteria have an important part in the licensing of LD reflexives in Mandarin. This has led some to the conclusion that there is a distinction between local binding of ziji which is syntactic and LD binding of ziji which is not. In particular, Reinhart and Reuland (1993), Xue, Pollard and Sag (1994), Huang and Liu (2001) conclude that reflexive binding is sometimes governed by syntax and sometimes by logophoricity. As researchers have shown that the completely syntactically unbound use of reflexives is undoubtedly possible, it would seem impossible to maintain that an exclusively syntactic model will suffice.

Therefore, a possible interpretation is to abandon movement accounts and conclude that LD reflexives are logophoric pronouns when they are bound long distance (Maling, 1984; Reinhart and Reuland, 1993; Huang 1994; Huang and Liu 2001).

However, following the ideas of Reinhart (1983), and concerning the relation between syntax and semantics, Reuland and Sigurjonsdottir (1997) claim that there is a preference for the least costly interpretation process when it is available. Thus in their discussion of the LD binding of the Icelandic reflexive sig they argue that there is an economy principle in which semantic interpretation carries a cost. Thus, semantic interpretation is an additional cost to the cost of syntactic interpretation.

> an interpretation procedure that is able to capture the semantic generalizations…requires operations that are language independent and go beyond what can be stated in C_{HL} … If this assumption is correct, which seems quite reasonable, this comes down to claiming that there is a

separate semantic component among our cognitive faculties.
(Reuland, 2001: 352).

Therefore, if two expressions α and β receive the same value a then they may be assigned this value (a.) syntactically or (b.) semantically. Thus, if α and β can be linked syntactically, "chain formation creates one syntactic object" (2001: 353). However, if syntactic chain formation is not possible, but α and β are identical variables bound by the same operator then they can be co-valued semantically. This is shown in (60), where C refers to the syntactic chain and x is the variable.

(61) a.   **Interpretation**

                                     ↑

      Semantic objects x_1

                                     ↑

      Syntactic objects C_1 ← C_1

      Basic expressions   α   ...   β

(62) b.   **Interpretation**

                                     ↑

      Semantic objects   x1   ←   x1

                                   ↑   ↑

      Syntactic objects   C1   C2

      Basic expressions   α   ...   β

(adapted from Reuland, 2001:353).

If the syntactic and semantic components of interpretation are viewed as modular, then the economy principle will mean that a syntactic interpretation will be preferred. Semantic interpretation will entail an additional cost as the number of cross-modular operations increases. However, if a syntactic interpretation is unavailable then a semantic interpretation becomes available.

In their comparative analysis of two Chinese dialects, Mandarin and Teochew, Cole, Hermon and Lee (2001) argue for the position that LD reflexives have to meet both syntactic and logophoric requirements. They claim that there is evidence to show that blocking has both a syntactic and logophoric component. Their first argument is that the evidence from other languages supports the contention (Sung 1990, Cole et al. 1993) that blocking will not occur in languages that have overt verb agreement. This contention would seem to have no explanation if blocking was solely due to logophoricity. This would also seem to explain that the blocking effect is stronger when it violates both logophoric and syntactic constraints. This could explain the asymmetry noted above (as in sentences (36) and (37), repeated here as (62) and (63)):

(63) **Zhangsan$_i$ zhidao wo/ni$_j$ xihuan ziji$_{*i/j}$.**
Zhangsan know I/you like self.
"Zhangsan knows I/you like myself/yourself."

(64) **Wo/ni$_i$ zhidao Zhangsan$_j$ xihuan ziji$_{i/j}$.**
I/ you know Zhangsan likes self.
"I/ you know Zhangsan likes my/your/himself."

Consider a third sentence:

(65) **Zhangsan$_i$ zhidao Lisi$_j$ xihuan ziji$_{i/j}$.**
Zhangsan know I/you like self.
"Zhangsan knows Lisi likes himself."

Cole et al. (2001) argue that in such cases the matrix subject is more felicitous as an antecedent for ziji than it is in sentence (63). Thus, the coindexing of (63) might be more accurately rendered as:

(66) Wo/ni$_i$ zhidao Zhangsan$_j$ xihuan ziji$_{??i/j}$.

Thus, we have a hierarchy of acceptability ranging from when there is no blocking (sentence (64)) to where the blocking is just syntactic (sentence (63) or (65)) to the most unacceptable (sentence (62)), where blocking is both logophoric and syntactic.

As noted in Cole and Wang (1996) sentences with subjects that are possible antecedents create strong blocking effects. This, however, is not the case if the potential antecedent is a non-subject. This would be in accordance with expectations under a LF head-movement analysis. Developing this analysis, Cole et al. (2001) note that a mild blocking effect occurs in such sentences.

2.7 Summary

In this chapter various generative syntactic accounts of LD binding have been examined with particular emphasis on the LF head-movement account. Such accounts were shown to have an impressive ability to account for the range of phenomena associated with LD reflexives. However, as was pointed out, a series of criticisms suggest that a purely syntactic analysis of this area seems to be untenable. Despite this, there seems no conclusive evidence that requires the abandonment of the LF head-movement hypothesis. The argument was then made that semantic explanations based on the idea of logophoricity were able to account for various phenomena that could not be explained using the syntactic model. Finally, it was argued that the acceptance of this line of argument did not necessarily entail abandoning movement as an explanation for long-distance binding.

Therefore, the research in this study will adopt a set of assumptions combining head-movement at LF and logophoricity to give a conceptual framework to account for the behaviour of reflexives. The following chapter will examine previous research into the SLA of reflexives and try to ascertain if the data is consistent with this framework. The final chapters will describe empirical testing, both in the L1 and L2. The tests will be designed to see if the binding of reflexives can be adequately explained by this model in the L1 and whether, the behaviour of informants in the L2 can be explained by the transfer from the L1 or recourse to the syntactic and logophoric elements of the set of assumptions that have been adopted.

Notes

1. These conditions are restated as interpretive conditions:
   If α is an anaphor, interpret it as coreferential with a c-commanding phrase in the relevant local domain.
   If α is a pronominal, interpret it as disjoint from every c-commanding phrase in the relevant local domain.
   If α is an R-expression, interpret it as disjoint from every c-commanding phrase.
   (Chomsky, 1995: 211).

2. However, see Zribi-Hertz (1989), Reinhart and Reuland (1983), Baker (1995) for discussion of non- syntactically bound reflexives in English.

3. See Huang (2000) for an extensive selection of examples.

4. According to Wexler and Manzini the reflexive sig is associated with value (d), the reflexive sjálfan sig, with (a); and the pronominal hann, with value (c).

5. However, Newson (1990) proposes a deductive link between anaphors and pronominals in any given language.

6. Progovac following Chomsky (1981: 209) refers to the AGR of finite clauses as SUBJECT (or big subject).

7. The idea of head to head movement seems to have originated with Lebeaux (1983). Though this chapter concentrates on movement from I to I an alternative theory is that the reflexive is adjoined to an IP and from there is predicated on its antecedent (Huang and Tang (1991).

8. Chomsky (1986: 14) proposes that a non-L-marked category constitutes a barrier, whereas an L-marked category is never a barrier. L-marked is defined as:
   α L-marks β .

iff β agrees with the head of γ.

and γ is θ-governed by α.

9. Not all authors agree on the felicity of this sentence.

10. See Moskovsky (2004) for an analysis where 1st and 2nd person blocking is determined by structural features. Blocking for 3rd person pronouns is complicated by the operation of a discourse factor, i.e. avoid ambiguity.

11. There are three classes of pronouns in Mupun: Set A indicate disjoint reference with the subject of the matrix clause; Set B indicate coreference with the matrix subject; and Set C indicate coreference with the addressee of the matrix clause.

12. See Cole, Hermon and Lee (2001) for arguments that PIVOT is the requirement in Mandarin.

13. The symbol O is used by Chierchia to indicate operator. Thus, the reflexive, ziji is the natural language equivalent of the λ operator.

14. See Cole, Hermon and Lee (2001) p. 21 for example sentences to support their contention thatpostverbal objects cannot be the antecedent for the reflexive. In addition, p.22-23 has some speculation on how the apparent contradiction between Chierchia's semantic analysis and the syntactic analysis could be resolved.

· Chapter 3 ·

Research into the SLA of Reflexives

3.1 Introduction

In chapter 1 theories of SLA were examined and the question of the UG derived nature of the ILGs of L2 learners was discussed. Chapter 2 was concerned with theoretical models of binding, with emphases on the theories of head movement at LF and logophoric binding. In this chapter research into the SLA of binding of reflexives will be examined.

3.2 Why study the SLA of Binding?

There are several reasons that make studying binding a promising area in ascertaining the extent to which the mental grammars of language learners are UG constrained. Firstly, it is an area that has been extensively researched, both in L1 and L2. As was discussed in the preceding chapter, there is a body of theoretical work, as binding has been a key area of syntactic research.[1] As will be discussed below, there has also been a considerable amount of research into the SLA of reflexives. This means that there is extensive data in the literature describing reflexives in a variety of languages.

The abstract and complex nature of binding has also led researchers into this area. In addition, although different researchers have posited different analyses, it seems that there is evidence that L2 binding could be subject to syntactic constraints and that these must come from innate knowledge. This is because it would be difficult to explain L2 learners' knowledge of reflexives by resorting to working from correction and general problem solving, due to the fact that if a possible antecedent is present then a sentence is still interpretable, though not necessarily in a way consistent with what was intended. As Cook notes:

> *it means on the one hand, that no one will detect that a learner has made a mistake, on the other, that learners will never be able to discover their mistakes from sentences they hear as they will put the wrong interpretation on them.* (Cook, 1993:173).

Although this could be disputed to an extent, in that pragmatic and/or semantic considerations could in certain situations make it apparent that a learner was making a mistake in his or her choice of antecedent, it nevertheless seems true that this kind of mistake would often go undetected. For example, the following sentence could be interpreted as referring to Bob's suicide.

(1) *Alan$_i$ knew Bob killed himself$_i$.
   In addition, the evidence is that reflexives are rarely explicitly taught in L2 language classrooms and their coverage in textbooks is scant.[2]

Finally, binding research allows investigation of both language universals (such as Principle A) as well as specific language features.

3.3 Previous studies of the SLA of reflexives

In this chapter we will look at some of the research into the SLA of anaphora. However, although much of this research was undertaken in a generative framework, the particular syntactic models used were often not the same as in this study. In particular much of the research was constructed to test for cross-linguistic effects of differences in the Governing Category Parameter and Proper Antecedent Parameter of Wexler and Manzini (Wexler and Manzini, 1987; Manzini and Wexler, 1987) discussed in the last chapter. Thus, much of this work was concerned with the question of whether learners were resetting parameters in accordance with the subset relationship previously described (see section 2.3). As this study assumes an alternative model, some of the assumptions made no longer seem valid. Nevertheless, there is much of interest in these studies in terms of the answers they can offer to the following questions:

   (i)   Are L2 learners' grammars operating in a way which is or is not UG constrained?

  (ii) What actual binding does the grammar of L2 learners manifest?

 (iii) Do the studies offer any insights into or evidence in support of head-to-head movement at LF or logophoric binding?

 (iv) What do the tests used in these studies tell us about the appropriateness of methodologies for testing knowledge of reflexives?

Therefore, the detail from this research will be examined to see if it offers any insights into these questions.

In an early pilot study (Finer and Broselow, 1986) tested six Korean learners, using stimuli sentences which had to be matched to one of a pair of accompanying pictures. The assumption was that the Korean reflexive caki had the largest or marked setting "e" of the governing category parameter, whereas English reflexives had the smallest or unmarked setting "a" (see chapter 2.3). In their results they found that the local subject was chosen as the antecedent for a reflexive in the great majority of bi-clausal sentences. However there was a significant difference between sentences such as (2) and (3) where the reflexive was contained in a tensed or an infinitival subordinate clause (see figure 3.1):

(2) Mr. Fat thinks Mr. Thin will paint himself.

(3) Mr. Fat wants Mr. Thin to paint himself. (Finer and Broselow, 1986)

Figure 3.1 (Finer and Broselow, 1986).

	Local (%)	Non-local (%)	Either (%)
Tensed Clause	92	8	0
Infinitival Clause	58	37	4

These results were largely replicated[3] in later studies (Hirakawa, 1990; Broselow and Finer, 1991; Finer, 1991; Thomas, 1991). This distinction could be explained in the Wexler and Manzini model by positing that learners had adopted an intermediate governing category parameter setting of "c" or "d". Thus the grammar would be UG-constrained and would show that L2 learners were capable of resetting parameters. Later tests expanded on the type of structures tested, the variety of informants' L1s and the variety of languages tested.[4] Though different researchers had different interpretations, Thomas, probably, expressed the majority view at this time when she wrote that the work done in this area is consistent with the hypothesis that UG is available in second language acquisition, in that the generalizations that could be made about learners' interpretations of reflexives in an L2, "count as evidence that learners can set L2 parameters to values not instantiated in L1" (Thomas, 1993: 54).

However, by the mid 1990s the Wexler and Manzini model was losing favour for a combination of conceptual and empirical reasons.[5] Nevertheless, it is still possible to argue that as some languages manifest the distinction where LD binding is possible into an infinitival, but not a tensed clause, learners are showing evidence for a UG-sanctioned grammar which has properties not manifested in their L1. Thus, as neither L1 transfer nor   input from the target L2 provides an explanation for the grammars L2 learners arrive at, then the deduction was made that the learners' access to UG was being demonstrated. White (1996) made the observation that if learners from null-Agr languages (like Korean) recognized agreement in the L2, but transferred an L1 setting that allows LD binding of reflexives, then the infinitival/tensed distinction would be predicted.

Researchers like Bennet (1994), Bennett and Progovac (1998), working within the releativized subject approach of Progovac (1992, 1993), used a somewhat similar argument to explain why Serbo-Croatian learners of English made a similar distinction. In sentences like (4), which involve object-control verbs, learners allowed the reflexive herself   to be bound by the matrix subject Ann, which is not possible for native speakers, as the indices suggest:

(4) **Ann$_i$ forced Claire$_j$ [PRO$_j$ to talk about herself $_{*i/j}$].**

The analysis was that in sentences with object-control verbs, learners had assumed that reflexives were monomorphemic (i.e. X^o – see chapter 2.3) as in their L1. Crucially, though, object control structures are absent from Serbo-Croatian excluding L1 transfer as an explanation.[6] However, the acquisition of the fact that English allows object-control structures leads learners automatically to allow LD binding, consistent with them having grammars that are UG-constrained, and underdetermined, both by the L1 and by input from the L2.

The argument that ILGs are underdetermined can be developed by looking at Thomas's (1989) findings that Spanish learners accepted LD binding in English, even though Spanish reflexives are locally bound. In this study Spanish- and Chinese-speaking learners of English were asked to interpret sentences. Thomas, noted that in sentences containing a tensed subordinate clause only 60 % of reflexives were bound locally by the Spanish speakers; whereas, the Chinese speakers performed more like the native-speaking controls in selecting the local antecedent in 69% of their responses, despite the fact that LD binding is possible in their L1. Thus, again we have the situation where the L1 and the L2 do not appear to account fully for the ILGs. As White (1996) pointed out, the performance of the subjects could result from a misanalysis of English as a null-Agr language, based on its comparative lack of morphologically overt agreement compared with languages such as Spanish. In this analysis, a failure of the Spanish learners to incorporate the polymorphemic mature of English reflexives into their ILGs would allow LD binding in principle. Failure to recognize overt-Agr in English would then allow LD binding out of a tensed clause.[7]

A further argument in support of the contention that ILGs are UG-constrained is that there is evidence of structure dependency. Thomas (1991),[8] using a multiple-choice comprehension task, tested subjects on sentences with relative clauses where the local subject was not the linearly closest compared with sentences with a sentential complement:

(5) The man who John met wrote a story about himself.

(6) Mary heard that Sue told the doctor about herself.

The structurally local antecedent, the man in sentence (5) is not linearly the closest, but in sentence (6) Sue is both linearly and structurally the closest. Thomas argues that her results show that, "[i]n both sentence types overwhelming portions of each group select the LOCAL NP (defined structurally) and not the CLOSEST NP as the antecedent of the reflexive" (Thomas, 1991:   230).[9]

A possible counter-argument to the position that the evidence indicates that learners are operating with a UG-constrained grammar has been made by a variety of researchers (Thomas, 1993; Eckman , 1994; Wakabayashi, 1996). For example, Wakabayashi used a task where informants were asked to judge the acceptability of all NPs in a sentence as antecedents for the reflexive. He notes that 12 out of 40 Japanese-speaking learners of English had ILGs which exhibited both LD binding and no subject orientation. This could be seen as problematic for Manzini and Wexler's hypothesis as, "an anaphor must be bound either in its unmarked governing category or by its unmarked proper antecedent" Manzini and Wexler (1987: 437). However, they emphasize that this observation is only tentative and that support for it is from empirical evidence rather than theoretical considerations. However, this area has been the focus of considerable interest in later studies conducted within the head-movement account because of the potential implications for binding theories.

The head-movement account explains LD binding by postulating that monomorphemic reflexives move at LF to I, where only the subject c-commands the reflexive. As movement is possible from head to head it is then possible for such a reflexive to be interpreted with an antecedent in a higher clause. Hence, there is a correlation between domain and orientation, in that only subjects can act as antecedents in such cases. Christie and Lantolf (1998) used cluster analysis to ascertain if there was such a correlation in the ILGs of learners of English and Chinese. Their hypothesis was that if ILGs did not show such a correlation then they were not sanctioned by UG. They claimed that their study showed evidence for non-UG sanctioned ILGs in some of their informants. However, as was pointed out by Thomas (1995, 1998), there is only a one way implication between domain and orientation. Thus, LD binding implies subject antecedent, but not vice versa. Similarly, object antecedents require local binding, but local binding does not necessitate object antecedents. Christie and Lantolf's analysis of learners who allowed LD binding, but also allowed either a subject or object antecedent, prompted White (2003) to comment on this and the similar conclusions of Eckman (1994) that, "they conclude, incorrectly, that the grammar is wild" (2003: 48) (see also Eckman 1994).

As Thomas (1995) notes, though object antecedents for LD reflexives may not be acceptable in some languages and/or for some lexical items, UG does not preclude local object antecedents for LD reflexives; examples include sebe in Serbo-Croat (Bennett, 1994) or propia in Italian (Giorgi, 1984). Thus, as Thomas (1995) argued it is necessary to exclusively use antecedents that are not clause mates of the reflexive in order to test the correlation between non-local binding and subject orientation. In her test of L2 learners of Japanese Thomas found that 30% the participants who allowed LD binding also permitted LD object antecedents in bi-clausal sentences. This is problematic for head-to- head movement as, "If long-distance binding entails subject orientation (as implied by movement in LF), it is not clear how a learner could attribute the first property to zibun but not the second property" (1995: 227).

Thomas argues that this is, perhaps due to a misanalysis of zibun as a pronoun. However, White (2003) notes that unless this analysis of the reflexive being interpreted as a pronoun is experimentally verified then it is unfalsifiable. Nevertheless, it is interesting that the rate of UG-illicit ILGs is much higher for low-level learners, with only 9% of the high-level learners accepting both LD reflexives and non-subject antecedents (see figure 3.2). As 10% of the native-speaking controls also allowed such an illicit correlation, there would seem to be evidence that the high-level learner who acquired the first property of LD binding also acquired the second, subject orientation. This interpretation gains some support from results from Yuan (1998) who found that only 6% of Chinese learners consistently allowed this "illicit" correlation.

Figure 3.2 % of respondents who allow LD binding
and % of thoserespondents who only allow subject orientation.
(adapted from Thomas, 1995)

L2 Groups	N	LD domain	N	LD domain + LD subject orientation
Low	34	35%	12	50%
High	24	46%	11	91%
Native Speakers	34	85%	29	90%

3.3.1 Criticisms

Though much has been learned from studies into the SLA of reflexives there are grounds to dispute some of the results and conclusions due to conceptual and empirical factors. This section will look at some of these problems.

3.3.2 Assumptions

In studying the status of UG in the SLA of reflexives it is necessary to have typological and theoretical knowledge of reflexives, both in the L1 and L2. However, when examining empirical studies in this area it is clear that certain assumptions that have been made are not that robust. Thus Broselow and Finer's analysis of Korean learners of English suggests that the setting of the Governing Category Parameter in their L1 is "e" (i.e. a language where reflexives are bound within the domain of a root tense, and therefore, have LD antecedents). Similarly, for example, Thomas (1991), in her study of the SLA of Japanese, bases her analysis on the X^o Japanese and Chinese reflexives zibun and ziji. However, as with Korean, both languages have polymorphemic reflexive forms[10] with syntactic behaviour that is analogous to English reflexives. Therefore, arguments based on the L2 learners changing parameters can be challenged on the grounds that the L2 parameters may already be extant in the L1. Yuan (1994), studying the SLA of English, argues:

> *if these learners can recognize English reflexives as phrasal reflexives by the surface form, then it is possible for them to generalize the behavior of the phrasal reflexive in their L1s to reflexives in English* (1994: 543).

Even if all the reflexives in an L1 are taken account of it can be argued that the lack of empirical validation of the binding behaviour attributed to these reflexives makes any conclusions drawn vis-à-vis the differences between L1 and L2 binding less definitive. Labov (1975) examined judgment data, on a range of different structures, and found extensive evidence of disagreements among informants. In addition, he

found many discrepancies between interpretations recorded in the
linguistic literature and the interpretations of linguistically naïve
informants. In addition it is also possible that dialect and even idiolect
variability could be significant in sentence assessment (Carden, 1970).
Finally, there is not always a consensus in the linguistic literature about
the binding behaviour of reflexives, with different authors giving
different interpretations of possible antecedents for reflexives.[11]
Therefore, it seems that a methodology which is asymmetric in
assessing the L1 and L2 leads to the increased possibility of
experimental variables distorting the relations between the L1 and L2
data.

Another frequently occurring problem seems to be uncertainty
about whether, in fact, the performance associated with the tests
actually shows instantiation of particular settings in the language. Thus,
Finer (1991) obtained the following results for Hindi-Urdu, Japanese
and Korean speakers interpreting antecedents in single-clause English
sentences:

Figure 3.3 (adapted from Finer 1991).

L1	Object (%)	Subject (%)	Ambiguous (%)
Hindi-Urdu	2	96	2
Japanese	21	78	1
Korean	19	81	0

These results appear puzzling because the results from other structures
tested showed the Hindi-Urdu speakers making judgments that showed
they "may have been native speakers of a form of English" (1991: 354).
As the assumption is that the antecedents in such sentences are
ambiguous the "responses of our Japanese and Korean speakers...
more closely mirror what the grammar of English would predict"
(1991:363). As Finer notes, Goodluck and Birch (1988) found 98% of

native-speakers of American English chose subject antecedents in a similar picture identification test. Thus, we are in the apparent position that native speaker judgments do not correspond to "English grammar". This problem is also shown by Hirakawa (1990) who employed a native-speaking control group. In this test, informants were asked to respond to sentences by indicating the correct antecedent. In single clause sentences, where informants were given the choice of selecting the subject, the object or both, only 12% of this group selected the "correct" response, either the subject or the object, while 21% selected only the object antecedent as possible. As the requirements for c-command are not met, it would seem, if we accept these data at face value, that either the native speakers are operating with a non-UG grammar or that binding theory is fundamentally flawed. This seems to cast into doubt the validity of any conclusions drawn on the tests.

3.3.3 Preferences

As several authors have pointed out (Thomas 1993, White et al 1998, Akiyama 2002) one interpretation for some of the idiosyncratic data obtained is that the tests are revealing preferences, rather than information about grammaticality, as determined by the subjects" grammars. Thus, the fact that, for example, 21% (Hirakawa, 1990) of native-speaking controls chose the local object antecedent as the only acceptable antecedent in single-clause sentences does not mean that their grammars prohibit non-local subjects in such sentences. Although, intuitively, this explanation seems to be the most reasonable, as presumably, the alternative is to postulate that native speakers in her experiment demonstrated the operation of three distinct grammars, it is still in some ways unsatisfactory. Firstly, if the evaluation is that the data from the control group expresses preferences then it seems untenable to maintain that the L2 learners' data is not doing the same.

This, therefore, compromises any conclusions that can be drawn about their ILGs. In addition, it is an ad hoc solution and really has no empirical support.

As White et al. (1997) and others have argued, both native speakers and L2 learners fail to detect more than one antecedent when a sentence is ambiguous. Thus, ambiguity leads subjects to reject interpretations where a possible antecedent is not the preferred choice. Thus, in a sentence with a local subject and local object, both are grammatical as antecedents of a reflexive in English:

(7) **John$_i$ told Bill$_j$ about himself$_{i/j}$.**

However, many studies show that the interpretation where the local object, Bill is the antecedent is rejected by L2 learners (Finer and Broselow, 1986; Hirakawa, 1990; Eckman 1994). However White et al. (1997: 146) question whether this, "failure reflects a property of the grammar (a competence phenomenon) or whether it relates to tasks (a performance phenomenon)." Thus, the danger in this case is that the linguistic competence of the L2 learners will be underestimated, if performance factors lead them to reject local binding of objects. As data from native-speaking controls has also failed to elicit the "correct" ambiguous response from a majority[12] this concern seems well founded.

The problem of eliciting preference judgments was recognised early on and several researchers have tried to counter it. Thomas (1991) and Matsumura (1994) and Bennet (1994) tried to train participants in the potential possibility of ambiguity. Wakabayashi's (1996) test design called for preference judgments on all potential antecedents, rather than selecting the correct antecedent(s). White et al. (1997) ran concurrent tasks to try and improve testing methodology. Thomas (1995) and Akiyama (2002), following work by Crain and McKee (1986) which showed that truth-value judgment tasks were capable of eliciting acceptance of the non-preferred analysis if a suitable context was provided, sought judgments based on contexts provided by stories.

3.3.4 Language Issues

There are reasons to be skeptical about some of the results so far obtained in this area due to possible problems with the language used in empirical tests. Hamilton (1996) makes the claim that LD binding could be over-reported as:

> *subjects sometimes resort to (perhaps partially informed) guessing responses because they cannot process or do not understand the structure of test stimuli, or because they are otherwise unable to follow the task directions.*
>
> Hamilton (1996: 438).

As he notes random answers would lead to a number of "apparent" LD responses. He cites evidence from Hirakawa (1990) and Matsumura (1994) showing LD binding is more common in three-clause sentences compared to two-clause sentences.[13] In addition, it has been noted that infinitival sentences may be more difficult to process than finite sentences. Cook (1990) found that Romance, Japanese and Norwegian learners of L2 English, as well as making more errors on infinitival compared to tensed sentences, also took longer in their timed responses.[14] Matsumura (1994) reported that certain subjects had to be dropped from her test due to their inability to process infinitival sentences. Thus, it could be argued that the pattern of greater acceptance of LD binding with infinitival clauses could be (at least partially) due to such processing difficulties.

Further problems could be due to the particular vocabulary used. Firstly, there has been debate about some of the verbs used, as it is possible there is often a preferred interpretation, based more on pragmatic and semantic, rather than syntactic factors. For example, Lakshmanan and Teranishi (1994) note that bi-clausal sentences with verbs such as hit, love or hate in the embedded clause would seem to naturally take the LD antecedent, "in the absence of additional context" (1994: 193). Demirci (2000) presented Turkish-speaking learners of English with pragmatically biased and neutral sentences and claimed that in bi-clausal sentences 69% of respondents chose the local antecedent when the sentence was pragmatically neutral, but when the sentence was pragmatically biased to the LD antecedent 83% of respondents then interpreted the antecedent as the long distance NP in sentences such as:

(8) The president ordered a bodyguard to protect himself carefullyduring the speech. (Demirci, 2000: 336)

Demirci concludes that the results for neutral sentences indicate

> *that many Turkish learners show evidence of a syntactic interpretation of English reflexives. However, ... these 79 learners readily relinquish the syntactic interpretation in pragmatically biased sentences.*

(Demirci, 2000: 347)

However, Thomas (1989) also contrasted pragmatically biased and neutral sentences. Though there was some effect from this her results were far less marked. Thus, only 34% of Chinese learners and 37% of Spanish learners chose the non-local NP when it was pragmatically favoured. Yuan (1998) looked at Chinese learners' acceptance of subject (licit) and object (illicit) antecedents in single-clause sentences. Three pragmatically favoured types were employed: subject favoured, object favoured and neutral. The results for the advanced group of learners' were that the acceptance of syntactically illicit object antecedents went from 13% (subject favoured) to 21% (neutral) to 32% (object favoured). As this means 68- 87% of responses were the grammatically licit subject, it seems to suggest that the results from Demirci's study are atypical, to the extent that learners "readily relinquish the syntactic interpretation." It is possible that this could be due to the lower English level of Demirci's informants. Thus, Yuan's results from the intermediate group (26%, subject favoured; 28% neutral; 52% object favoured) are perhaps more in line with Demirci's. However, without comparable data on the groups this cannot be verified.

Hamilton (1996, 1998) argues from the position that logophoricity can explain apparent incidents of non-syntactic LD binding. As previous empirical studies had generally not considered logophoricity[15] his argument is that evidence for syntactic LD binding can only be accepted "if it can be shown that learners... do not utilize a logophoric binding strategy in the L2 to any significant degree" (1996: 433).

Hamilton (1998) tested Japanese learners of English to see if he could detect logophoric binding. Following the analysis of Reinhart and Reuland (1993) and Pollard and Sag (1992, 1994), only when the reflexive is not bound to a referential coargument of the predicate to which it belongs is it free to take logophoric antecedents. Thus, "binding for polymorphemic reflexives is ... seen to be a last-resort phenomenon" (1998: 303) that is only available when syntactic binding does not apply (i.e. it is not bound in its governing category). Hamilton, using a truth-value judgment task, asked his informants to judge the acceptability of sentences matched with accompanying pictures that forced a non-local antecedent interpretation. The sentences were divided into two types: exempt and non-exempt exemplified in sentences (9) and (10).

(9) Miss Grey$_i$ reported that Miss Young spilled water on John and herself$_j$.

70

(10) Miss Old$_i$ reported that Miss Young sprayed herself$_i$ with water.

(Hamilton, 1998: 308)

Hamilton found that when the anaphor is in a non-exempt position (such as in sentence (9) where herself is a co-argument of the predicate headed by sprayed) then 12.9% of the Japanese informants' responses were acceptances; this compared to a 18.7% acceptance rate for the exempt stimuli. As native-speaking controls accepted 4.4% of non-exempt and 18.4 % of exempt stimuli and, based on an analysis that Japanese lacks such logophoric binding, Hamilton argued that was evidence of access to UG.

Although Hamilton's results are interesting, a criticism could be made that all the sentences in his tests allowed the possibility of logophoric binding, in that the non-local antecedents in all the stimuli could be seen as meeting the logophoric requirements posited by Sells and Chierchia outlined in chapter 2. As 81.6% of the exempt stimuli were rejected by the native-speakers, it could be argued that the evidence is not that they are free to be logophorically bound as they are not syntactically bound by virtue of not being coarguments of the predicate. An alternative interpretation would be that syntactic binding applies to all the stimuli. However, logophoric binding is more likely to be accepted in non-exempt stimuli because generally they are more difficult to process due to the fact that the reflexive is not the direct bare object of the verb, but is embedded within a co-ordinate structure or a picture NP or PP etc.

3.3.5 Empirical Issues

Criticisms can be made of many of the studies in this field due to empirical issues. The first criticism is that, in many cases, insufficient attention seems to have been paid to ensuring that the tokens employed in the test are objectively as valid as possible. Though most studies have employed more than one token to represent syntactic types it is often the case that a limited number of tokens, often employing some of the same lexis have been used. For, example, Akiyama's experimental design included the stipulation that, "the verb that takes an infinitival clause as its complement was restricted to the verb want" (2002: 33). Though this was logical in trying to avoid problems associated with object-control verbs[16] it does raise questions about how much can be inferred about the syntax from studying a single lexical item. As Cowart (1997: 6) comments, "lexical differences between different tokens can produce quite substantial differences in judged acceptability." This could be an (at least partial) explanation for some of the discrepancies in results between studies.

The second criticism has been the apparent disregard for the possibility of context effects skewing the results. One recurring omission in the literature is the absence of filler sentences. If such sentences are omitted this could potentially compromise the reliability of the data. Akiyama is one of the few who mentions this subject. However, his distracter sentences numbered only 2 and both contained reflexives. His claim that they served to, "distract participants' attention from the target structure" (2002: 35) is open to dispute as the target structure is a reflexive in a bi-clausal sentence so it could be argued that the participants' attention is being drawn to reflexives. If informants can deduce the kinds of sentences the experiment is concerned with by, for example, detecting repeated patterns, this means there is a possibility "they will adopt response strategies that are unrepresentative of their general behavior" (Cowart: 1997: 52). In addition, the syntactic processing and evaluation of sentences can be based on preceding sentences (Bock 1990). Thus, a research methodology, which presents sentences testing binding judgments in a set order, is potentially inducing judgments which are a function of the test methodology and are thus, potentially not automatically applicable to drawing more general conclusions. Similarly, the pretesting and pretraining (Thomas, 1989; Bennett and Progovac 1998; Akiyama, 2002) that has involved anaphors could also be pertinent to their strategies in subsequent testing. As researchers are presumably trying to gather data on the underlying ILGs of participants there is a real danger that such methodological issues could have real and unpredictable effects on results.

Finally, as Wakabayashi (1996) noted there are limitations in analyzing aggregate response data. Such data does not reveal the individual's ILG,[17] though aggregate data can be regarded as characteristic of a group if it is homogeneous. However, it is often possible to question the homogeneity of some of the groups in previous studies based on their linguistic backgrounds and their language levels. It would thus seem unsafe to reach conclusions on the systematic knowledge individuals have based on data from heterogeneous groups.

3.4 Summary

Though there have been claims in the literature, it seems that there is no decisive evidence that non-UG-sanctioned ILGs are permissible. Although evidence from various studies has led researchers to claim the availability of UG in SLA these claims, based on knowledge of the binding possibilities of reflexives underdetermined by input are still controversial. There are still sufficient doubts about the conceptual framework and the validity of experimental methodology that conclusions drawn from ensuing data cannot yet be seen as conclusive. Therefore, the next chapter will look at the specific languages and outline the methodology employed in this study in an attempt to elicit data which can present further insight in this field.

Notes

1. See Lees and Kilma (1963), Jackendoff (1972) and Kuno (1972) for early work in this area

2. Thomas (1993) reports that her survey of six teachers and a dozen textbooks found that coverage of this area was at best brief or vague. Akiyama(2002) reported similar results from his survey.

3. As with Finer and Broselow (1986), a difference between the interpretation of infinitival and tensed clauses has been a consistent finding in the research literature.

4. Much of the early work was based on the L2 acquisition of English. However, there has also been research into Japanese (Thomas, 1991, 1993, 1995), Chinese (Yuan, 1998) and Spanish (Christie 1992).

5. See MacLaughlin (1995) for a criticism of the Wexler and Manzini model.

6. Hamilton points out that from the perspective of the LF head-movement account, "it is not clear that Agr is the determining factor for establishing binding domains" (1996: 428).

7. See MacLaughlin (1998). She argues that 7 out of 15 native-speakers of Chinese and Japanese allow binding out of infinitival clauses as they recognize overt Agr, but have failed to recognize the polymorphemic nature of English reflexives.

8. See also Akiyama (2002).

9. See O'Grady (1996) for arguments that evidence of c-command in L2 is consistent with non-access to UG.

10. Yuan (1994: 541) provides a list of phrasal reflexives in Chinese, Korean and Japanese which he states can only be bound locally.

11. Examples from the literature include:
    (i) Zhangsan de baba de qian bei ziji de pengyou touzou le.
        Zhangsan DE father DE money BEI self DE friend steal
        PERF.
        "Zhangsan's father's money was stolen by his friend."
        (Tang, 1989: 104).
        According to Tang (89) baba is the only possible
        antecedent, but Xu (1994) also accepts Zhangsan.

    If we compare:
    (ii) Zhangsani renwei woj zhidao Wangwuk xihuan
         ziji*i/*j/k.
         Zhangsan think I know Wangwu like self.
         "Zhangsan thinks I know Wangwu likes himself." (Cole
         and Sung, 1994: 372)

    with:
    (iii) Johni juede woj zhidao Markk xihuan ziji*i/j/k.
          John think I know Mark like self.
          "John thinks I know Mark likes me/himself." (Pan,
          2001: 298)

    Cole and Sung maintain that, "when an immediately higher
    subject differs in person from a lower subject, LD reflexives
    are blocked" (1994: 363). However, Pan allows 1st and 2nd
    person pronouns to be antecedents in this (very) similar
    sentence.
12. Native-speaking responses of "ambiguous" were under 50 %
    in all the tests mentioned with the exception of Lakshmanan
    and Teranishi (1994) who report 58%.

13. LD binding rates for two and three clause sentences (Hamilton (1996: 439)).

	Level	Type	Two clause %	Three clause %
Hirakawa (1990)		Tensed	23	32
		Infinitival	44	46
Matsumura (1994)	Low	Tensed	31	42
	Low	Infinitival	49	56
	High	Tensed	19	21
	High	Infinitival	33	24

14. Response times and error rates for infinitival and tensed two clause sentences in English containing a reflexive (1990: 582-583).

L1	Type	Error rate %	Response time seconds
Japanese	Tensed	23.4	6.979
	Infinitival	40.6	7.180
Romance	Tensed	7.1	6.723
	Infinitival	30.4	7.720
Norwegian	Tensed	2.9	6.558
	Infinitival	19.1	6.316

15. Thomas (1995) did discuss the possibility of logophoric binding and raised the possibility that some of her data might be, " reanalysed as evidence of learners' sensitivity to the logophoric properties of zibun" (1995: 231). However, her test did not test this as all logocentric NPs were also structurally legitimate.

16. Akiyama (2002) noted that the use of object control verbs could be problematic. As PRO is within the same clause as the reflexive the assumption is that selection of Claire as the antecedent demonstrates local binding. However Akiyama argues that there is the possibility of learners directly interpreting the antecedent as the object of the main clause. This would then lead to analysis of LD binding as the antecedent is now not a clause mate of the reflexive. This problem could be compounded if the learners ILG has yet to develop PRO in which case Claire and herself could again be viewed as clause mates. Thus, Akiyama argues that "studies in which (object) control verbs are used... face a serious conceptual problem" (2002: 31).

17. Akiyama (2002) makes the point that Finer's (1991) analysis of learners' ILGs as position c of the GCP it would require showing that individuals consistently performing accurately on sentences with embedded finite clauses and poorly on those with embedded infinitival clauses. He comments that, "the aggregate data did not show the existence of such participants" (2002: 32).

Second language acquisition of English reflexives
by Taiwanese speakers of Mandarin Chinese

• Chapter 4 •

Considerations in Test Design

4.1 Introduction

The next three chapters are concerned with empirical testing of reflexives. This chapter will examine theoretical and practical considerations that were taken into account in the design and implementation of these tests. First, the methodology of testing will be examined. Second, issues arising from the nature of language will be discussed, with an emphasis on the factors that are pertinent to the particular languages relevant to this study. Finally, this chapter will examine the pilot tests which were designed to provide information on binding in Mandarin Chinese and Taiwanese[1].

4.2 Methodological Issues

Research into the acquisition of languages has been carried out using a variety of different methodologies. In the area of the SLA of reflexives most research has been conducted through comprehension tasks where informants have been asked to evaluate in some way sentences containing the target structure or structures. Though such experimental methodology is not without problems, alternative methodologies of trying to elicit production or observing natural occurrences of the structures are possibly even more problematic. In this section differing methodologies will be discussed and evaluated.

4.2.1 Production Tasks

The design of production tasks to elicit knowledge about learner competence must confront the problem that it is by no means certain that production can be equated with competence. Some researchers have suggested that learners' productive language could lag behind their knowledge (Izumi, 2003). Furthermore, if production were a perfect reflection of competence, it might be expected that L2 learner performance in production and comprehension would be isomorphic. But it is not clear that this is the case. Thus Kempe and MacWhinney (1998) acknowledge they can make no claims about production based on testing comprehension as, "the distributional characteristics relevant for comprehension and for production may well differ" (1998: 581). If there is such a difference, then it could be argued that claims about comprehension based on production data cannot be made with any degree of confidence.

A second difficulty is that designing stimuli to elicit target structures is difficult because of the often complex nature of the target structures themselves and the possibility of using non-target structures in response to the stimuli. As Thomas (1995:66) notes, "It is hard to design an experimental paradigm narrow enough to elicit the precise target structures, but broad enough to allow subjects to display their virtuosity." Hamilton (1998) used a sentence completion task with sentences such as:

> **(1) Mr Short found _____ in the picture.**
> **(Hamilton, 1998: 308)**

80

Accompanying the sentence was a drawing depicting "Mr Short pointing to himself in a photograph and saying, "[t]here I am!" (1998: 308). This task was designed to screen participants to test their knowledge of English reflexive forms.2 However, there appears to be no research which has attempted to move beyond this extremely controlled and limited production task.

4.2.2 Observation

Researchers in this field of reflexive binding have also eschewed methodologies based upon observation of natural occurrences of learners' production of the relevant structure. This is due to a variety of factors. First, there is the problem that failure to produce a structure is not evidence of the absence of knowledge of that structure in the ILG. Thus, the performance of the individual is not necessarily providing us with a full picture of their competence (see Cook, 1990). This problem is compounded by the rarity of the target reflexive structures in most discourse situations, with the consequence that practical considerations would often preclude an observational methodology.

4.2.3 Comprehension Tasks

Because of the methodological problems associated with using production tasks to investigate L2 knowledge of reflexives, researchers have used a variety of comprehension tasks to try and elicit speakers' evaluation of antecedents. A number of studies have used a multiple choice task where participants select antecedents from a set (Hirakawa, 1989, Thomas, 1991, Matsumura, 1994). Similarly, picture identification tasks have asked participants to select from a range of pictures designed to show different interpretations of the binding of the reflexive (Finer and Broselow,1986, Bennet, 1994, Eckman, 1994). However, as many authors have pointed out, there is a considerable amount of doubt as to whether these methods really inform us of the true extent of learners' ILGs. Wakabayashi (1996: 272) notes that when a possible interpretation is arrived at, subjects "may stop the process of interpretation." Thus if there is more than one interpretation available, whether in the grammar of a native speaker or the ILG of a learner, this would not be apparent in the data. Though attempts have been made to overcome this problem by pre-training subjects in ambiguity (Thomas, 1991, Bennet, 1994) the efficacy of such methods has not been demonstrated. White et al. (1997) note that English native speakers will sometimes reject non-subject antecedents in mono-clausal sentences:

> *they will recognize the object interpretation if it is pointed out to them or if the context favours it. In some cases, however, their preference may be so strong that it overrides perception of any other interpretation; they may not notice or may reject the interpretation ... Even so, the fact that they choose only one interpretation does not necessarily mean that the other is excluded from their grammar.* (1997: 148).

In an attempt to overcome the perceived difficulties of such comprehension tasks researchers have also employed "truth-value judgment tasks" (Crain and McKee, 1986). In such tasks a context is provided and participants are asked to determine if an accompanying sentence is appropriate. A number of different methods have been use to provide a context, the two most common being stories (White et al, 1997; Akiyama, 2002) and pictures (Thomas 1995, Christie and Lantolf, 1998, Hamilton, 1998). However, it is not clear that truth-value judgment tasks can be taken as overcoming the problems associated with ambiguity and the elicitation of preferences (see White et al. 1997).

Wakabayashi (1996) used a preference ordering task in an attempt to overcome some of the evaluation difficulties found in other studies. Figure 4.1 shows the format of the questions used in this study.

Figure 4.1 Question Design (Wakabayashi, 1996: 274).

Sentence: Tom told Sam that the police would arrest him.
Question: Who is him?

Tom	Sam	Someone not mentioned	I don't know

In this sentence, him can mean Tom or Sam or Someone not mentioned.

If you prefer Sam to Tom or Someone not mentioned your answer will be:

Tom	Sam	Someone not mentioned	I don't know
2	1	3	

If you prefer Sam to Tom and Someone not mentioned your answer will be:

Tom	Sam	Someone not mentioned	I don't know
2	1	2	

If you don't prefer any of them, and think that it totally depends on the ontext, your answer will be:

Tom	Sam	Someone not mentioned	I don't know
1	1	1	

If you think the ordering of the preference is very difficult, please use the last pattern in order to indicate all possible answers.

In addition, subjects were presented with a list of all the NPs after each question and asked whether each NP was a possible antecedent. Wakabayashi claims that his experiment, "tapped subjects" competence more deeply than previous studies by encouraging subjects to indicate all possible antecedents" (1996: 279).

4.3 Testing in the L1

Much of the research in this area, and indeed in SLA, has followed the methodology of testing informants in the L2, but relying on a theoretical description of the relevant L1 grammar. If it is assumed that the particular structure is well understood and described, uniformly adhered to by native speakers who will uniformly give interpretations consistent with the understood grammar, then such a methodology can be defended. However, it is far from clear that this is the case in the present study which is concerned with the acquisition of L2 English reflexives by native speakers of Mandarin Chinese (hereafter referred to as Mandarin).[3] In this case it can be argued that the assumptions posited above are not met because of disagreements about the actual behaviour of Mandarin reflexives, uncertainty about the full range of UG options instantiated in the informants of this study and by the fact that previous testing of reflexives provides evidence that informants cannot be uniformly relied upon to behave in ways consistent with theoretical grammatical models.

Thus, a criticism of Finer and Broselow's pioneering 1986 study is that it lacked native-speaking L2 controls. Though, they have been employed in most later studies many researchers have commented on the fact that it became clear that native-speakers did not always concur with what theoretical-linguistic descriptions claim are and are not acceptable antecedents for reflexives. This problem is compounded in that testing methodology cannot be guaranteed to always elicit what researchers anticipated. Thus, it is clear that without such controls analysis based on L2 learners' interpretations is subject to additional uncertainty.

However, it can also be argued that a similar uncertainty is introduced into any final analysis if the L1 is not also tested. Thus, an assumption that learners have a particular L1 grammar is only an assumption if it is not empirically verified. Therefore, a key premise underlying the use of native-speaking controls is that the judgment of the researcher is inadequate due to factors such as (inadvertent) bias, their linguistic knowledge and dialectal differences. Thus, the arguments for empirical verification in the L2 can also be employed for the L1.

4.4 Language Background

Though there is an extensive literature on the binding of reflexives in Mandarin (Tang, 1989, Xu 1994; Pan 1997; Liu 2003 and others) it is still necessary to ascertain if the informants' grammars are consistent with those described in the literature. First, it needs to be noted that although there is a consensus on much of the behaviour of reflexives in Mandarin there are still areas where there is dispute both about what are, and what are not, permissible antecedents for reflexives in certain structures.[4] A possible source of explanation for this variability could be dialectal variation among speakers. Thus, for example Cole et al. (2001: 33) question whether their, "picture of Mandarin... is peculiar to Singapore .... or whether it is true as well in the Mandarin heartland, northern China." This sensitivity to the possibility of dialect differences has rarely been acknowledged in the literature. However, as all informants in this test were residents of Taiwan it was necessary to take this factor into account, as there was a possibility that the published accounts of the grammar of reflexives in "standard" Mandarin would not apply to the case of speakers in Taiwan.

In testing Mandarin speakers from Taiwan it is necessary to have an appreciation of the linguistic environment. First, there has been a degree of political, geographic and cultural isolation from other speakers of Mandarin, particularly from those living in what is usually seen as the home of standard Mandarin, the People's Republic of China. Thus, as would be expected, there is clear evidence of phonetic and lexical divergence. In addition, there is also some evidence that there are now grammatical differences.[5] However, this is an area in which it is hard to make assertions, as the research data is limited, and we could add, is also an area which is possibly changing quite rapidly.

A second major issue is that Taiwan is far from being monolingual. Though Mandarin is an official language, and until relatively recently other languages were proscribed and censured in certain public and official contexts, native speakers of other languages continue to exist in significant numbers. Thus, a native speaker of Mandarin might well have a second native language. The most prevalent of these native languages is Taiwanese. This language is spoken by approximately 80% of the population.[6] In addition, other languages are also spoken. However, even if our testing was to concentrate on the approximately 20% of the population who maintain they are purely Mandarin speakers it is not clear if it is tenable to assume that such individuals are truly monolingual. In addition to the influence Taiwanese has had on the dialect of Taiwanese Mandarin, the widespread use of Taiwanese in advertising, the media, and in recent years, some educational and government contexts, means that it would be possible to argue that all residents of Taiwan are, to at least some extent, likely to have some knowledge of Taiwanese. Thus, if assertions are made about their L2 competence based on L1 Mandarin, there is a possibility of experimental error based on the existence of a different instantiation of UG. As this knowledge is a continuum, ranging from those who are effectively bilingual to those with, for example, a limited knowledge of some lexical items etc. it is difficult to disentangle the effects of the two languages on each other. Thus, if the grammar of Taiwanese was different from that of Mandarin it could potentially invalidate any claims made about the properties of the informants' ILGs.

The particular circumstances on Taiwan possibly exacerbate a more general conclusion that the linguistic homogeneity of a group of speakers of language X should not be assumed.

A third potential threat to the accuracy of an analysis of data collected from speakers in Taiwan is that the notion of "word" has a different status in the writing systems of the L1 and L2, a fact that may influence informants' judgments involving written elicitation methods. Chao (1968) notes that sociological and linguistic words are often not the same in Mandarin. Sociological words in Chinese are defined in terms of characters. However, linguistic words may be made up of one or more characters. In English there is a high degree of overlap between the two notions, but this is often not the case in Chinese. The Chinese writing system does not mark word boundaries but individual morphemes. However as Chen and Zhou (1999) note:

> *words are transparent units for speakers of European languages. However, it is not obvious whether the same arguments and conclusions relating to word processing that have been reached through psycholinguistic studies with European languages can be generalized to other languages, such as Chinese, in which words are not transparent units.* (pp. 425-426)

Empirical support for this seems to come from studies which have shown inconsistency between native speakers when they are asked to mark word boundaries on text (Hoosian 1991). Although Packard (2000) argues that the syntactic representation is the most salient it is not clear that this can be assumed for testing purposes. Thus, if we take the example of the "word" taziji, himself, herself. This could be viewed as a compound word equivalent to English himself, herself, or as the pronoun ta "he, she" and the compound word ziji, "self" or even as the three separate words, ta, "he, she", zi, "self" and ji, "self". Thus, Tang (1985) and others have noted there is a possible ambiguity as taziji may be interpreted as a polymorphemic locally bound reflexive or a pronoun modified by an emphatic reflexive. This contrast is shown in sentences (1) and (2).

(1) **Zhangsan$_i$ renwei taziji$_{i/*j}$ hui qu.**
Zhangsan think himself will go
"Zhangsan thought that himself would go." (sic)

(2) **Zhangsan$_i$ renwei ta$_j$ ziji$_{i/j}$ hui qu.**
Zhangsan think he self will go
"Zhangsan thought that he himself would go." (Tang, 1989: 98)

Further evidence that ta can be interpreted as a pronoun comes from the apparent felicity of sentences where the blocking effect and the local nature of monomorphemic reflexives would preclude blocking, for example:

(3) **Zongton$_i$ qing wo$_j$ zuo zai ta ziji$_{i/*j}$ de   shenbian.**
President askme sit at he self DE side.
"The president asked me to sit at his side." (Cole, Hermom and Huang 2001:17)

4.5 Concluding remarks on previous studies

This study takes as a premise that an accurate knowledge of the informants' L1 is necessary in order to ascertain what their ILGs tell us bout their access to linguistic knowledge. Therefore, informants are tested in both Mandarin and English. However, because of the informants' language background pilot tests were conducted to determine whether assumptions made based on Mandarin as the L1 were still valid in light of the informants' knowledge of Taiwanese. Thus, the pilot tests were principally designed to see if binding in Taiwanese differed from that of Mandarin. More detailed testing of the informants' L1 is presented in chapter 5 and similarly detailed testing of their knowledge of the L2 in chapter 6.

As was discussed in section 4.2, empirical methods have been subject to various criticisms. Although the minimizing of experimental error is an obvious goal, it seems clear that its total elimination is not a realistic possibility. As can be seen from previous tests, it would appear that control of all variables in this area of research is a goal which is hard to achieve. Though efforts are made to control variables it would seem to be unrealistic to claim that all variables have been taken account of. Therefore, a variety of tests are employed to try and ameliorate the possible effects of testing methodology on the data.

The tests use comprehension tasks. For the pilot tests a grammaticality judgment task was used. However, informants were asked to rate all potential antecedents on a scale as to their acceptability.[7] The aim was to allow informants the option of giving an intermediate rating to a non-preferred antecedent rather than having to either reject or accept it. Following Wakabayashi (1996), it was hoped to tap learner competence more directly. A similar methodology was used in the main tests in Mandarin and English. However, in the main tests in Mandarin, this was preceded by a more conventional grammaticality judgment task where informants were asked if an interpretation was acceptable. This was done in order to be able to cross-check the results. Thus, if unanticipated test design factors were skewing results in one test this would be apparent from the differing results in the other test. In addition, the specific nature of the questions concerning antecedents and the quantity of judgments that have to be made if all NPs in a sentence are to be rated, mean that practical considerations make it very difficult to try and disguise the focus of the research from informants. The use of filler sentences in the conventional tests means that the focus of research is much less transparent. Finally, a truth-value judgment task, based on a series of pictures was employed in the English tests.

4.6 Pilot Tests

This section describes experiments investigating binding in L1 Mandarin and Taiwanese. Two parallel tests were run in the respective languages, with identical methodologies and formats. This was done to ascertain whether a distinction needed to be made between speakers of these languages when examining their ILGs in the L2.

4.6.1 Subjects

The subject pool consisted of 51 undergraduate students at Shih Chien University in Taiwan. All subjects were nationals of Taiwan. The majority of the subjects were females in their early 20s. Subjects were sub-classified based on a pre-test screening of their access to other languages using a self assessment-form. The results of this are shown in Figure 4.2.

Figure 4.2 Language known by informants

Language	Native speaker	Fluent	Competent	Poor
Mandarin	51			
Taiwanese	33	7		11
Other "Taiwanese" Language	4	2	1	

Subjects who were speakers of other languages were eliminated. In addition, those subjects who indicated their Taiwanese was fluent or competent were also eliminated. This was done to try and maintain a clear distinction between a bilingual Taiwanese/ Mandarin group and a monolingual Mandarin group. Therefore, the final data pool consisted of 44 informants. The informants were divided into two groups. Group A consisted of 22 subjects randomly selected from the bilingual group. This group was tested in Taiwanese. The remaining bilingual subjects were assigned to group B with the eleven monolingual subjects and tested in Mandarin.

4.6.2 The test stimuli

Test sentences were designed to determine whether the claims about reflexive binding attested in the literature were reflected in the intuitions of speakers from Taiwan. All written material and all test items were presented in Chinese script only. Various facets of the behaviour of the reflexive ziji were investigated. Thus, this pilot test was designed to see if the behaviour exhibited by the informants was consistent with the anticipated binding patterns of reflexives. Parallel tests were undertaken for the Taiwanese monomorphemic reflexive gadi. The test stimuli were designed to see if speakers:

(i)   allowed long-distance (LD) binding of the reflexive.
(ii) only accepted subject orientation.
(iii) exhibited syntactic blocking.
(iv) showed evidence of non-syntactic blocking.

The subjects were asked for their interpretations of reflexives in three different sentence types. All the sentences were exactly duplicated between the tests in Mandarin and Taiwanese.[8]

Type 1

Tri-clausal sentences with the reflexive in the subordinate clause.

(1) a. **Shiming tingshuo Wenxiang renwei Xiaoming taoyan ziji.**
Shiming hear Wenxiang think Xiaoming hate self.
"Shiming hears Wenxiang thinks Xiaoming hates him/ himself."

   b. **Shiming tiagong Wenxiang lingwee Xiaoming touya gadi.**
Shiming hear Wenxiang think Xiaoming hate self.
"Shiming hears Wenxiang thinks Xiaoming hates him/ himself."

In this sentence ((1) a. in Mandarin and b. in Taiwanese) all the NPs are considered possible antecedents for the reflexive as they are all subjects which c-command the reflexive. In Type 1 sentences acceptance of any antecedent apart from the local NP (Xiaoming in sentence (1)) indicates that LD binding is permissible in grammars of the respective languages. In addition, by changing the 3rd person NPs to 1st or 2nd person pronominals it is possible to see if the blocking effect is manifested if antecedents in higher clauses are blocked. As any change in features between the NP in the local clause and NPs in higher clauses will be syntactically blocked, it is not possible to purely look at non-syntactic blocking (i.e. logophoricity) in this sentence type. However, it is possible to contrast sentences where blocking of NPs is (i) syntactic and (ii) both syntactic and non-syntactic. This is shown in sentences (2) and (3), where the difference in features in both sentences syntactically blocks LD binding. However, only in sentence (3) does the local NP lead to non-syntactic blocking of the NP in the matrix clause.

(2) **Nirenwei Xiaoming taoyan ziji.**
     You think Xiaoming hate self.
     "You think Xiaoming hates himself."

(3) **Wenxiang renwei ni taoyan ziji.**
     Wenxiang think you hate self.
     "Wenxiang thinks you hate yourself."

Type 2

Biclausal sentences with the reflexive in the embedded clause.

(4) **Kexin yiwei Xiaoyu xihuan ziji.**
     Kexin assume Xiaoyu like self.
     "Kexin assumes Xiaoyu likes her/ herself."

In this sentence type there is a choice between a local and LD antecedent. In the head-movement account the LD antecedent will only be available if there is no conflict in   features (as in sentence (4)).

Type 3

Bi-clausal sentences with a subject and non-subject NP in the matrix clause.

> (5) **Wenxiu renwei Daian gaosu guo Kexin youguan ziji de gongzuo.**
> **Wenxiu think Daian tell GUO Kexin about self DE job.**
> **"Wenxiu thinks Daian told Kexin about his job."**

Type 3 sentences offer two subject NPs; in addition, there is also a non-subject NP. Thus, following the head-movement hypothesis the two subject NPs are both permissible candidates to be the antecedent for the reflexive. However, the non-subject NP is not. If the features of the non-subject NP do not agree (as in sentence (6)) then any blocking of the LD antecedent would not be syntactic.

> (6) **Wenxiu gaosu wo Kexin dui ziji you xinxin.**
> **Wenxiu tell me Kexin to self have confidence.**
> **"Wenxiu tells me Kexin has confidence in her/herself."**

Type 4

Biclausal sentences with a clause containing a sub-commanding NP.

> (7) **Xiaoyu renwei Xiuling de xuesheng taoyan ziji.**
> **Xiaoyu think Xiuling DE student hate self.**
> **"Xiaoyu thinks Xiuling's student hates her/ herself."**

Type 4 sentences include two NPs which c-command the reflexive. However, in the embedded clause, only the head of the NP c-commands the reflexive. Thus, in sentence (7) xuesheng is the local antecedent. Therefore, as the 2nd person pronominal in sentence (8) is not a head the LD antecedent is not syntactically blocked. Therefore, any blocking of the LD antecedent can be interpreted as non-syntactic blocking.

(8) **Xiaoyu renwei ni de xuesheng taoyan ziji.**
Xiaoyu think you DE student hate self.
"Xiaoyu thinks your student hates her/ herself."

4.6.3 Testing

In the test session subjects were presented with 10 sentences all including a reflexive. The sentences were presented in a random order. In addition, they were also asked to judge the acceptability of an unspecified extra-sentential NP as a potential antecedent. The subjects were instructed to rate all NPs on a scale with 1 being assigned to candidates that were completely natural and normal. A 5 rating was assigned to candidates that were not possible in any circumstances. Subjects were instructed to give intermediate rating (i.e 2, 3, 4) for NPs they judged to be in between (see Figure 4.3). These instructions were presented verbally, when the task was being introduced, and were repeated in written instructions given to the informants.

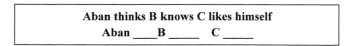

Figure 4.3 Example of test question
(actual test questions used Chinese script only)

4.6.4 Results

Figure 4.4 Mean scores for NPs

Type of NP	Blocking	Mandarin (non-proficient in Taiwanese)	Mandarin (Taiwanese speakers)	Mandarin (Totals)	Taiwanese
LD NP		1.76	1.93	1.91	1.89
Local NP		1.63	1.57	1.61	1.54
LD NP	Syntactic	2.55	2.20	2.38	2.45
LD NP	Syntactic & non-syntactic	2.72	2.91	2.82	2.86
LD NP	Non-syntactic	2.32	3.02	2.68	2.28
Non c-commanding NP		4.01	3.93	3.97	3.85
extra-sentential		4.39	4.27	4.33	4.67

All NPs that were present in the test stimuli were classified, based on whether they were c-commanding or non c-commanding. C-commanding NPs were then divided into local and long-distance, with LD NPs being sub-classified depending upon whether and what kind of blocking effects were applicable. In addition, the data for non-specified extra-sentential NPs was collected. This was done independently for the Taiwanese group and the Mandarin group. However, the results from the monolingual-Mandarin group and the bilingual- Mandarin group were also collated and analysed separately. Figure 4.4 gives the means for each kind of NP.

The results show the means for each of the groups for all instances of candidate NPs in the test stimuli. Independent ANOVA analysis failed to indicate any significant difference between the groups in their responses.[9] This was true for all of the candidate NPs.

However, when the groups' results for different types of NPs were examined significant differences were found. Repeated-measures one-way ANOVA were performed. There was a significant difference between mean judgment scores: $F(6, 126) = 14.59$, $p < 0.01$ for Mandarin and $F(6,126) = 17.03$, $p < 0.01$ for Taiwanese. Post hoc Scheffé tests indicated significant differences in Mandarin ($p < 0.05$) between the ratings for local antecedent and all the other categories, with the exception of licit LD NPs and the syntactically blocked NPs. As the former are held to be licit in Mandarin this result would not be unexpected. However, the fact that no significant difference was found with the latter could be viewed as not supporting the model of binding adopted by this study. The explanation for this could be that as a purely syntactically blocked NP has to be a 1st or 2nd person pronoun (as a blocked 3rd person pronoun is also blocked non-syntactically) then the semantic salience of such pronouns means that the effects of syntactic blocking are somewhat masked. These results were replicated in Taiwanese ($p < 0.05$) with the one exception being that no significant difference was found between non-syntactically blocked NPs and local NPs.

4.6.5 Concluding remarks on the pilot tests

There was clear evidence that LD binding of reflexives was permissible both in Mandarin and Taiwanese. When syntactic and non-syntactic factors did not conflict with such an interpretation there was no significant difference between the acceptance rate for the local and LD antecedent.

Similarly non c-commanding antecedents were far less acceptable to both groups and significant differences were shown to exist for both language groups between antecedents which c-commanded the reflexive and both objects and non-heads as well as extra-sentential antecedents. However, it is worth noting that a minority of respondents (3 in the Mandarin group and 2 in the Taiwanese group) consistently accepted extra-sentential antecedents.

Though there were significant differences between local NPs and blocked LD NPs, the evidence was less definitive. Therefore, the results did not offer counter-evidence to the hypotheses concerning blocking; however, more refined and extensive testing would be needed.

Finally, these results failed to show any differences between Mandarin and Taiwanese with respect to the binding of reflexives. There was also no difference detected in the way Taiwanese and non-Taiwanese speakers responded to stimuli in Mandarin.

4.7 Summary

In this chapter, it was argued that a potential shortcoming in previous SLA research was the inadequacy of data on the L1 of informants. The assumption that a particular grammar describes the L1 of informants was held to be problematic if it had not been experimentally verified. This problem could be especially salient in the present study, where the informants were residents of Taiwan, with Mandarin as their L1. The possibility of dialectic variation from "standard" Mandarin meant that it could not be assumed that the literature provided an accurate representation of the informants' grammar. Furthermore, the widespread knowledge and usage of Taiwanese meant that an assumption that the UG instantiated in Mandarin described the linguistic knowledge of the informants was untenable.

The pilot tests were designed to examine Taiwanese and Mandarin, with respect to the binding of reflexives. This was done to determine if the grammars of these two languages treated reflexives in the same way. The test results for Mandarin showed that the both the Taiwanese-speaking and non-Taiwanese-speaking informants allowed the LD binding of reflexives, were disinclined to accept non c-c-commanding antecedents and exhibited blocking. In addition, no significant difference was found between Mandarin and Taiwanese. Thus, it seems that varying degrees of Mandarin/ Taiwanese bilingualism can be excluded as an extraneous variable in the main tests.

Notes

1. Taiwanese refers to the dialect of Min Nan Chinese spoken in Taiwan.
2. Interestingly two (out of 45) of the native-speaking controls were screened for, "producing instances of her self, him self or them selves (with a clear space between the determiner and self, suggesting that the subject analysed the reflexive as two separate words" (Hamilton, 1998: 312).
3. So far, in line with much of the linguistic literature, this study has used the terms Mandarin and Chinese interchangeably. However, as Mandarin is just one of the dialects or languages covered by the term Chinese in order to avoid possible confusion the term Mandarin will now be used exclusively.
4. See footnote 11 Chapter 3 for examples of different interpretations about permissible antecedents for reflevives.
5. See Cheng (1985) for a discussion of the differences between "Peking Mandarin" and the Mandarin spoken in Taiwan.
6. This figure is taken from Cheng (1985). Other sources give slightly lower percentages. See Wikipedia (http://en.wikipedia.org/wiki/Taiwanese_(linguistics)).
7. See Cowart (1996) for discussion of treating results from scale measurements as interval data for the purposes of statistical analysis.
8. All sentences employed identical lexis and word order. They were checked with native-speaking informants to ensure that they were grammatical and not stylistically awkward.
9. $F(2,41) = 0.57$

• Chapter 5 •

L1 Testing of Reflexives in Mandarin

5.1 Introduction

In this chapter experiments investigating binding in L1 Mandarin are described. The next chapter will describe experiments investigating both non-native and native English. The same subject pool of Mandarin speakers was used in both sets of tests. Thus, this chapter attempts to ascertain the nature of informants' L1 grammars with respect to binding. Any conclusions subsequently drawn about their ILGs in the L2 will benefit from a clear picture of binding properties in the subjects' L1 grammars. In order to obtain as objective a measure of binding properties in the L1 as possible, and to reduce the possibility of experimental design skewing the results, two different tests were administered to the same subject pool.

5.2 Subjects

The original subject pool consisted of 112 undergraduate-university students from Taiwan. All subjects were studying English. As with the pilot tests, all subjects were nationals of Taiwan and native-speakers of Mandarin. The subjects were all linguistically naïve. Prior to testing subjects completed a self-assessment questionnaire.

Details of the language backgrounds are given in Figures 5.1 and 5.2. The 15 subjects who had proficiency in languages other than Mandarin, Taiwanese and English were excluded. Figure 5.2 gives details of the age and sex of the remaining 97 subjects.

Figure 5.1 Language Background

Languages	Self-assessed fluency			
	Native Speaker	Good	Some	None/ a few words
Mandarin	112	-	-	-
Taiwanese	71	13	3	25
Other	9	4	2	11

Figure 5.2 Age and sex of subject pool

Age	Female n = 79	Male n = 18
Mean	21.6	21.2
Range	20-32	20-24

5.3 Test Stimuli

Six different types of sentence were used in the tests. As with the pilot tests, all written material and all test items were presented in Chinese script only. Type 1 to Type 3 were the same as in the preliminary test (see section 4.7 for discussion). They are repeated below:

Type 1

Tri-clausal sentences with the reflexive in the subordinate clause.

(1) **Shiming tingshuo Wenxiang renwei Xiaoming taoyan ziji.**
    Shiming hear Wenxiang think Xiaoming hate self.
    "Shiming hears Wenxiang thinks Xiaoming hates him/ himself."

Type 2

Bi-clausal sentences with the reflexive in the subordinate clause.

(2) **Meifeng zhidao Aban xihuan ziji.**
    Meifeng know Aban like self.
    "Meifeng knows Aban likes him/ himself."

Type 3

Biclausal sentences with a sub-commanding potential antecedent.

(3) **Xiaoyu renwei Xiuling de xuesheng taoyan ziji.**
    Xiaoyu think Xiuling DE student hate self.
    "Xiaoyu thinks Xiuling's student hates her/ herself."

In addition, three further sentence types were included in these tests:

Type 4

Bi-clausal sentences with a verb in the matrix clause indicating the subject of that clause has no knowledge of the proposition of the embedded clause which contains the reflexive.

(4) **Xiuling bu zhidao Afang taoyan ziji.**
    Xiuling not know Afang hate self.
    "Xiuling doesn't know Afang hates her/ herself."

In these sentences all NPs c-command the reflexive and are, therefore, potential antecedents for the reflexive. If, however, there is a requirement of SELF or SOURCE (Sells, 1987) or self-ascription (Lewis, 1979; Chierchia, 1989) then the subject of the matrix clause would not meet it (see section 2.5.2 for further discussion).

Type 5

Bi-clausal sentences with a subject and object in the subordinate clause containing the reflexive.

> **(5) Wenxiang renwei Aban gaosu guo Shiming youguan ziji pengyou de shiqing.**
> **Wenxiang think Aban tell GUO Shiming about self friend DE affairs.**
> **"Wenxiang thinks Aban told Shiming about his friend's affairs."**

In these sentences both the subjects in the matrix and subordinate clause c-command the reflexive. Acceptance of the subject in the matrix clause in sentence (5) (i.e. Wenxiang) indicates LD binding. In addition, syntactic and non-syntactic blocking can be examined by changing the subject or the object in the subordinate clause so their features do not match with those of the subject of the matrix clause. In sentence (6) any blocking is non-syntactic as the reflexive can still move from the head in the subordinate clause to the head of the matrix clause.

> **(6) Wenxiang renwei Aban gaosu guo ni youguan ziji pengyou de shiqing.**
> **Wenxiang think Aban tell GUO you about self friend DE affairs.**

"Wenxiang thinks Aban told you about his/ your friend's affairs."

However, in sentence (7) the subject of the matrix clause is blocked both syntactically and non-syntactically as movement is blocked through the intervening first person head.

(7) **Wenxiang renwei wo gaosu guoShiming youguan ziji pengyou de shiqing.**
Wenxiang think I tell GUO Shiming about self friend DE affairs.
"Wenxiang thinks I told Shiming about his/ my friend's affairs."

Finally, in sentence (8) any blocking of the subject of the matrix clause is purely syntactic.

(8) **Ni renwei Aban gaosu guo Shiming youguan ziji pengyou de shiqing.**
You think Aban tell GUO Shiming about self friend DE affairs.
"You think Aban told Shiming about your/ his friend's affairs."

In the tests only sentences corresponding to sentences (6) and (7) were used, as practical considerations limited the number of stimuli. As data on non-blocked local and LD antecedents was available (from sentence Type 1, 2, 3, 4 and 6 stimuli), sentence (5) was omitted. Similarly, no test item corresponded with sentence (8), as sentence Type 1, 3, 4, and 6 stimuli provided data on syntactic blocking,

Type 6

Uni-clausal sentences with a subject and object, and containing the reflexive in a complement phrase.

(9) Kexin wen Afang yoguan ziji pengyou de shiqing.
Kexin ask Afang about self friend DE affairs.
"Kexin asks Afang about his friend's affairs."

In these sentences, there is both a subject and an object. However, if subjects are the only permissible antecedents for monomorphemic reflexives then the reflexive cannot be bound by the object.

In the two tests that were run a total of 38 sentences relevant to the focus of this research were used: 21 in test 1 (see Appendix 1) and 17 in test 2 (see Appendix 2). Thirty four contained the monomorphemic reflexive ziji, with the other four containing taziji. Figure 5.3 shows the breakdown for the number of stimuli used in each test.

Figure 5.3 Number of stimuli by sentence type

Sentence Type	Test 1	Test 2	Total
1	6	5	11
2	1	1	2
3	4	4	8
4	3	3	6
5	2	0	2
6	5	4	9
All	21	17	38

5.4 Test Descriptions

Two tests were conducted. Test 1 was designed to elicit the preferred antecedent. Test 2 asked the informants to give grammaticality judgments on antecedents in a variety of sentences. The target reflex sentence stimuli were duplicated in both tests. Though this had the disadvantage of restricting the total number of different stimuli used, uniform structure and lexis had the advantage that possibly unforeseen idiosyncratic features associated with particular structures or lexical items would not complicate analysis. In addition, the lexis was restricted to relatively frequent everyday items due to the fact that the English test stimuli were designed to be as close as possible to the Mandarin ones. This was to reduce the possibility of responses being the result of ignorance on the part of L2 learners of particular lexical items in the English tests. Thus, for example, the Mandarin tests used only simple verbs like *tingshuo,* "to hear", *zhidao*, "to know", *renwei*, "to think" etc.

5.4.1 Test 1

Test 1 comprised 53 sentences; 21 sentences were concerned with the binding of reflexives and were, therefore, relevant to this research. The remaining sentences were fillers, used to distract from the focus of the research. In Test 1 informants were presented with a sentence, and were then asked to determine which of the following stimuli best shared the same meaning as the test sentence. For example, subjects were shown sentences such as (10) and were then asked to select either (10 a.) or (10 b.).

(10) Xiuling wangji le Afang taoyan ziji.
Xiuling forget LE Afang hate self.
"Xiuling has forgotten Afang hates her/ herself."

a. Afang taoyan Xiuling.
Afang hate Xiuling.
"Afang hates Xiuling."

b. Afang taoyan Afang
Afang hate Afang.
"Afang hates Afang."

All test sentences were grammatical. However some of the associated following stimuli were possibly grammatically dubious.[1] This was necessary so as to avoid use of target structures in these stimuli. For example, in sentence (10 b.) to preclude having to use the target reflexive, *ziji* the use of the r-expression, *Afang* is bound to an r-expression. However, native-speaking informants stated that the meanings of such stimuli were clear. The design of this test did not allow the informants to select more than one answer. Therefore, the informants are being tested on their "preferred" interpretation. This means that if an alternative interpretation is available this is not recorded. The test was designed in this way for a variety of reasons. First, problems associated with trying to elicit the full range of sentence subjects deemed to be grammatical, rather than their preferences mean that there is no guarantee that the researcher has truly obtained the desired data (see section 3.3.3 for further discussion). Researchers such as Thomas (1991) and Bennett and Progovac (1998) have, with mixed results, tried to overcome this problem by giving pre-testing instructions on ambiguity. However, it is open to doubt whether they have entirely succeeded. In addition, the problems associated with the notion of what a "word" is in

Chinese languages (discussed in Section 4.4) could lead to unanticipated bias in any results. As Tang (1989) and others have noted, *taziji* can be viewed as a pronominal, with a monomorphemic reflexive emphasizer or as a polymorphemic reflexive. This could mean that overt instruction in finding ambiguity could lead to informants indicating ambiguity when it might not be warranted, as it would be possible to analyze compound words in a variety of ways. This combined with the abstract and de-contextualized nature of the stimuli in a testing framework means that it would be possible to question the reliability of non-preferred elicited stimuli. Therefore, no pre-training was given to the informants. Finally, the format of the test allowed filler sentences to be included so that the focus of research could be obscured from the informants.

The remaining 32 sentences were filler, used in order to distract from the focus of this research. The filler sentences were designed to vary from being fairly clear to very ambiguous. Thus, as much as possible the level of ambiguity in the filler sentences was designed to mirror that of the sentences being tested. Respondents, interviewed after the test reported that prior to Test 2 they were unaware that there was an emphasis on reflexives.

5.4.2 Test 2

Test 2 presented the informants with 16 sentences. No filler sentences were used, as the amount of time necessary for respondents to complete a test with a sufficient number of filler sentences would have been prohibitive. The format of the questions is shown in Figure 5.4.

Figure 5.4 Test 2: question format

Xiuling wangji le Afang taoyan ziji.

    Xiuling [   ]   **Afang** [   ]

Xiuling forget LE Afang hate self

    Xiuling [   ]   **Afang** [   ]

Informants were asked to rate whether each of the NPs in the question sentence could refer to the reflexive. Thus, in the example in Figure 5.4 they were asked to assign a rating to both the matrix subject, Xiuling and the embedded subject, Afang. In this test, a 7-point scale was employed.[2] A rating of 1 was to be given to antecedents which were "perfectly natural and acceptable" and a rating of 7 to those that were "not possible". If the acceptability fell somewhere between these two interpretations, informants were instructed to use intermediate scores of 2-6.

5.4.3 Testing Procedures

The subjects were all enrolled at Shih Chien University in Taipei. Participation was voluntary and subjects were told they were helping with research into how people learn language. No specific details were given about the focus of the research until it was completed. Participation in the research allowed the volunteers to enter a lottery with 12 prizes; the prizes were all valued at about £10. The subjects were split into four groups and tested in four different sessions. Though the questions were identical in each session, the order of questions was randomly selected for each of the four groups.[3] Thus, any effect of question order would be mitigated.

The tests were run in a single session. Test 1 preceded Test 2 in order to try and ensure the focus on reflexives was initially not made obvious. Prior to both tests informants were given written instructions in Mandarin and oral instructions in English. The test was then presented and subjects were allowed up to 20 minutes to complete Test 1. After completing Test 1 subjects were then given further instructions before commencing Test 2 which took 20- 25 minutes to complete.

5.5 Results

Figures 5.5 and 5.6 give the results for LD subject antecedents for the monomorphemic reflexive, *ziji*. These results were collected from all sentence types with the exception of Type 4 sentences.[4] All subject antecedents in the test stimuli were classified as to whether there was any potential blocking. Where all the NPs were third person and there was, therefore, no potential for blocking (i.e. "no blocking" in Figures 5.5 and 5.6), then such antecedents were selected as the preferred option 76.5 % of the time in Test 1. The grammaticality judgment task in Test 2 resulted in a mean score of 2.25 (recall that informants were asked to rate possible antecedents on a scale going from 1 "perfectly natural and acceptable" to 7 "not possible"). A repeated measures two-tailed t-test was performed and no significant difference was found between LD and local antecedents ($p > 0.05$). This would seem to confirm that LD binding is readily accepted in the grammars of the informants.

However when a candidate LD antecedent NP was third person, but an intervening potential antecedent was first or second person (i.e.

"syntactic and non-syntactic blocking" in Figures 5.5 and 5.6) it was the preferred choice in only 16.8% of cases in Test1, with a mean of 3.9 in Test 2. The results are also shown in Figures 5.5 and 5.6, for those cases where a candidate LD antecedent was first or second person, but an intermediate NP was third person (i.e. "syntactic blocking"), and when the a candidate third person LD antecedent was contained within a sentence which contained a first or second person NP, which did not c-command the reflexive (i.e. "non-syntactic blocking").

A purely syntactic account would predict that the results for "no blocking" and "non-syntactic blocking" would be the same. Similarly, a syntactic account would predict no differences between "syntactic blocking" and "syntactic and non-syntactic blocking".

Figure 5.5 Test 1:
showing % preferences for LD subject antecedents (ziji)

Blocking	Range	Mean %
No	61.7- 97.9[5]	76.5
Syntactic & Non-syntactic	7.3- 28.0	16.8
Syntactic	42.4- 63.8	52.1
Non-syntactic	28.6-47.0	35.9

Figure 5.6 Test 2:
showing mean grammaticality judgments forLD subject antecedents (ziji)

Blocking	Range	Mean
None	1.59- 2.59	2.25
Syntactic & Non-syntactic	2.84-4.46	3.90
Syntactic	2.30- 2.89	2.56
Non-syntactic	2.24- 3.12	2.71

However, when blocking was involved, the presence of a purely syntactic "blocker" did not seem to fully account for the results. ANOVA testing was performed and there was a significant difference between mean judgment scores: $F(3,388) = 17.20$, $p < 0.01$. Post hoc Sheffé tests showed there was a significant difference ($p < 0.05$) between those instances where blocking was caused by an intervening first or second person subject (indicated as syntactic and non-syntactic blocking in figures 5.5 and 5.6) and those where an intervening third person pronoun syntactically blocked access to a first or second person subject (indicated as syntactic blocking). Non-syntactic blocking seemed to also be a factor. In sentences which contained a first or second person NP which was not in a subject position and did not, therefore, syntactically block LD antecedents such antecedents seemed to be less felicitous. Again, a significant difference was observed between such sentences and those where there was no potential blocking ($p < 0.05$). In addition, there was also a significant difference between these and those where blocking was both syntactic and non-syntactic ($p < 0.05$). However, no significant difference was found when blocking was only syntactic.

Comparing these results with those for *taziji* we find that they do not emphatically support the view that as a polymorphemic reflexive LD binding should not be possible. LD antecedents, when there was no blocking, were the preferred choice in 37% of cases, with a mean of 2.55 in Test 2. Although a repeated measures t-test indicated there was a significant difference between *ziji* and *taziji* ($t = 3.62$, $p < 0.05$) there were still a relatively high number of subjects who selected the LD antecedent as the preferred choice. In addition, the grammaticality judgment score did not seem to indicate that such antecedents were clearly unacceptable. Thus, to many informants they were either grammatical or much more felicitous than might have been anticipated.

The results for non c-commanding NPs are shown in Figures 5.7 and 5.8. The results for third person NPs indicate that they are not acceptable as antecedents. They were very rarely the preferred option and the mean of 5.51 obtained in Test 2 shows they were generally judged as unacceptable[5]. However, when the stimulus was a first or second person NP there was a significant difference in the acceptability of such non c-commanding NPs: $t = 11.96$, $p < 0.05$.

Figure 5.7 Test 1:
showing % preferences for non c-commanding antecedents (ziji).

	tokens	range	mean %
3rd person	2	0-2.06	1.03
1st/ 2nd person	1	15.45	15.45

Figure 5.8 Test 2: showing mean grammaticality judgments
for non c-commanding antecedents (ziji).

Object	tokens	range	mean %
3rd person	2	5.09- 5.93	5.51
1st/ 2nd person	1	4.11	4.11

The results for object antecedents are shown in Figure 5.9 and 5.10. These results seem strongly to confirm the subject orientation of the monomorphemic reflexive, *ziji* when the object is a third person NP. However, the results for first and second person NPs are less definitive as though they were only the preferred choice 17.08% of the time they were grammatically judged to be considerably more acceptable than 3rd person NPs, with a mean of 2.68 ($t = 2.49$, $p < 0.05$).

For those sentences which contained the polymorphemic reflexive *taziji,* the object was selected as the preferred choice in 35% of cases and its mean grammaticality rating was 2.43. Therefore, the significant difference between these results and those for ziji would seem to offer support to the view that the polymorphemic reflexive can be bound locally to an object.

Figure 5.9 Test 1:
showing % preferences   for object antecedents (ziji).

Object	tokens	range	mean %
3rd person	5	0-2.06	1.3
1st/ 2nd person	2	11.46-22.68	17.08

Figure 5.10 Test 2:
showing mean grammaticality judgments for object antecedents (ziji).

Object	tokens	range	mean %
3rd person	5	3.89- 6.14	5.72
1st/ 2nd person	2	2.14-3.22	2.68

The results from the Type 4 sentences indicated that SELF or SOURCE, or *de se* requirements were not part of the grammars of speakers of Taiwanese Mandarin. The LD antecedent in such sentences was the preferred choice in 74% of the sentences and the grammaticality judgment mean was 2.18 These results were similar to corresponding sentences where the verb allowed the subject LD antecedent to meet these requirements and no significant difference was found ($p < 0.05$).

5.5.1 Results for taziji

The results for *taziji* appear to offer limited support for its analysis as a polymorphemic reflexive. First, if *taziji* and *ziji* are compared, for LD subject antecedents there was a significant difference. In test 1, only 37% of responses showed a preference for the LD antecedent with *taziji*, compared to the mean of 76.5% with *ziji*. Similarly in test 2, the grammaticality rating for *taziji* was 2.55, compared with a mean of 2.25 for *ziji*. However, though this does suggest that *taziji* is less felicitous as an LD reflexive, it does not seem to offer firm evidence that its LD binding is prohibited in the grammars of the informants. Furthermore, the large number of respondents who actually preferred the LD subject over more local subjects means it would be difficult to maintain an analysis of *taziji* as an X^{max} reflexive which is bound to its local head for those informants.

The results for object antecedents showed that *taziji* was more acceptable than *ziji*. In test 1 35% of responses showed a preference for the object antecedent with *taziji*, compared to a mean of 1.3% with *ziji*. In test 2, the grammaticality rating for *taziji* was 2.43, compared to a mean of 5.72 for *ziji*. These results would appear to offer better support for the analysis of *taziji* as a locally bound polymorphemic reflexive. However, as there was a limited number of test stimuli contained *taziji* (recall only 4 of the 38 relevant test sentences), caution must be employed.

5.6 Summary

The results of these tests were consistent with the pilot tests, in that they also indicated the acceptability of LD binding for the monomorphemic reflexive, *ziji*. In addition, they also confirmed the pilot tests, in that objects and non-heads which do not c-command the reflexive were generally not seen as preferred or acceptable antecedents. Thus, these results would be consistent with the literature on the binding of ziji and can be explained by a purely syntactic account of head movement.

However, when blocking was involved syntax seems to only account for some of the behaviour exhibited. Thus, the results could show a hierarchy of acceptability, shown schematically in Figure 5.11.

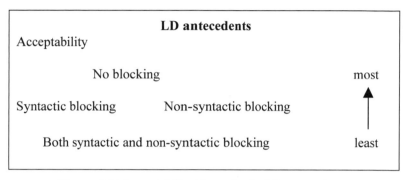

Figure 5.11 Acceptability hierarchy for LD antecedents.

Thus, only when the blocking is both syntactic and non-syntactic is an antecedent seen as fully ungrammatical. This would therefore, support the argument of Hermon and Lee (2001) that reflexives have both syntactic and logophoric requirements.

However, the evidence does not support the contention that Mandarin has either SELF or SOURCE requirements. Thus, the data suggests that Taiwanese Mandarin speakers show responses consistent with those claimed for Singaporean Mandarin speakers by Cole et al. (2001). In this analysis the antecedent is the centre of deixis and this would seem consistent with the results in this research. Cole et al. comment that:

> *The occurrence of a first or second person pronoun is taken to indicate that the speaker, rather than some internal protagonist is the center of deixis.* (Cole et al. 2001:12)

Thus the most readily acceptable antecedents in the hierarchy are those where there is no blocking. In such cases the LD antecedent is a possible PIVOT, as this NP can be seen as the internal protagonist who is the centre of deixis in the sentence. As movement from head to head is syntactically permissible the candidate NP is judged as an acceptable antecedent. However, syntactic blocking means that the candidate NP is the centre of deixis (due to being either first or second person) and is therefore favoured logophorically as the antecedent. However, as movement is blocked by the intervening head's divergent features it makes their interpretation as the antecedent less than totally felicitous. A similar lack of felicity results   when non-syntactic blocking means that the candidate NP is not favoured as the centre of deixis as the presence of a first or second person NP in the sentence acts as the PIVOT. However, because this first or second person NP is not an intervening head it does not block movement of the reflexive to the candidate NP under the head-movement account.   Finally, the blocking is most pronounced only when both the blocking of head movement by a difference in features in an intervening head and the presence of a first or second person NP acting as a PIVOT combine.

The results from *taziji* are also interesting in that a purely syntactic account would seem to be inadequate to account for the equivocal nature of the results if it is assumed that *taziji* is a polymorphemic reflexive. However, any conclusions drawn must be tentative, as the test design does not allow us to rule out the possibility that subjects were analyzing *taziji* as more than one word.

Notes

1. i.e. the use of a R-expression which is not free.
2. See Cowart (1996: 67-77) for a discussion on scaling issues in test design.
3. A random number generator   was used to determine question order in the four versions of the tests.
4. Although subsequent analysis of the data failed to detect any effects from verbs which precluded awareness Type 4 sentences were excluded as if such effects had been manifested they could have been an extraneous factor.
5. However, in common with the pilot tests, a small minority of respondents (i.e. six) consistently accepted such antecedents.

Second language acquisition of English reflexives
by Taiwanese speakers of Mandarin Chinese

· Chapter 6 ·

L2 Testing of Reflexives in English

6.1 Introduction

This chapter is concerned with experiments conducted in English. The principle aim of these experiments was to obtain a clear picture of how the learners interpreted reflexives in the L2. This "clear picture" would then be used to try to determine the role of UG in SLA and whether the model of head-movement and logophoricity presented in this study was adequate in accounting for the data.

The two experiments administered were a grammaticality judgment test and a truth-value judgment test. The Mandarin (and Taiwanese) speaking informants who participated in the tests described in the preceding chapter formed the main subject pool. As data was collected on the grammar of reflexives in their L1 these L1 grammars could, therefore, be compared to the English ILGs of the same informants in relation to the binding of reflexives.

6.2 Subjects

The main subject group consisted of the original subject pool of undergraduate university students from Shih Chien University in

Taiwan (see Section 5.2). Nineteen individuals from the original pool of 97 were unavailable and eight more were discarded for technical reasons associated with the experiment. This meant that 70 subjects completed these tests.[1] In addition, a native English-speaking control group also took part. This group consisted of 15 subjects: 7 from the U.S.A,; 5 from the U.K.; 2 from Canada and 1 from Australia. Though the native-speaking controls' educational levels were more varied than those of the Mandarin group they were all educated at college level and linguistically naïve. Background information was also collected on the age and sex of the control group and the details are shown in Figures 6.1 and 6.2. Thus, when we examine the subject pool in its entirety it consists primarily of tertiary-level educated females in their twenties.

Figure 6.1 Educational backgrounds of control group

Education	Number
Undergraduate	3
B.A. / B.Sc.	10
M.A./ M.Sc./ M.B.A.	2
Other	0

Figure 6.2 Age and sex of control group

Age	Female n= 9	Male n=6
Mean	26.2	25.7
Range	21.9- 33.6	20.8- 36.7

6.2.1 English Level

Information was also collected on the L2 group's exposure to English and their proficiency in the language. All individuals in this group were currently studying English at university and had also studied English in junior and senior high school. In addition, some individuals had also studied English in private cram schools either prior to and/ or concurrent with their education in the school system of Taiwan. None of the group had spent a significant amount of time in the target language (i.e. English-speaking) environment. Figure 6.3 shows the age of first exposure to and the duration of study of English.

Figure 6.3 Informants' exposure to English

	First exposure to L2	Years studying L2
Mean	11.35	8.7
Range	6-13	7.4-13.6

One potential criticism could be that a significant number of informants had exposure to the L2 prior to puberty. Following the arguments of Lenneberg (1967) this could compromise any data as it is possible that parameter resetting took place prior to puberty. However, it can be argued that two factors mitigate the significance of this. First, the amount and quality of the exposure to the L2 was extremely limited. Second, there appeared to be no evidence from such things as test results and interaction with the subjects in their current study of English that their performances were any different from their peers who had started their education in the L2 at a greater age. Nevertheless, a criticism could be that this view is largely subjective and not empirically validated. However, the decision was made to include the subjects with an early exposure to the L2. To try and ensure that this was not an erroneous decision, a post test analysis of the data was conducted to see if there were any differences between early and late exposure to English groups.[2]

In order to ascertain the current proficiency of the Mandarin speaking subjects they all completed a standardized test of English.

The Oxford Quick Placement Test was used.[3] The scores from this test were used to divide the informant pool into a lower level group and a higher level group.

6.3 Test Stimuli

In total seven different sentence types were used in the two tests. All sentences were in the simple past tense.

Type 1: multi-clausal sentences with the reflexive in a subordinate tensed clause

(1) Sally knew Becky painted herself.

The only grammatically licit antecedent for the reflexive *herself* is the local NP, *Becky*. Acceptance of the other NP, *Sally* would indicate an acceptance of LD binding. Following the analysis of Yang (1983), Pica (1984; 1987) and others (see section 2.5.1) *herself* is an X^{max} reflexive which cannot move from its immediate phrase, where it is interpreted. However, if such a sentence is judged as legitimate by informants this does not necessarily provide evidence that their grammars disallow LD binding as both NPs' features agree with those of the reflexive. If we compare sentence (1) with sentence (2):

(2) *Sally thought Tom hated herself.

The clash in features between the local NP, *Tom* and the reflexive, *herself* would not allow local binding (assuming the respective features are recognized). Therefore, if informants judged such a sentence grammatical it would seem to be because they are interpreting the long-distance NP, *Sally* as the antecedent of the reflexive. However, as *herself* is an X^{max} reflexive movement out of its clause is prohibited.

Type 2: bi-clausal sentences with a non-tensed subordinate clause containing a reflexive

(3) Jack wanted Tom to drive himself to school.

As with Type 1 sentences the X^{max} reflexive *himself* means that only the local NP, *Tom* is an acceptable antecedent. However, as many researchers have noted LD binding out of clauses, where the verb does not carry tense, is often more readily accepted.

As was noted by Akiyama (2002: 31) object control verbs can be problematic as it is conceivable that an informant could have failed to identify PRO and are long-distance binding the reflexive out of its immediate clause to the object of the main clause.[4] The contrast between the structures is shown in sentences (4) and (5).

(4) Jack persuaded Tom$_i$ [PRO$_i$ to drive himself to school.]
(5) Jack wanted [Tom to drive himself to school.]

Therefore, to avoid this potential cause of uncertainty only ECM verbs were used in Type 2 sentences.

Type 3: uni-clausal sentences with subject and non-subject NPs

(6) Becky asked Sally about herself.

In sentence (6) the reflexive does not move to I and stays within the VP. Thus, as well as the subject NP (*Becky*), the non-subject NP (*Sally*) is a possible antecedent. Though both NPs in sentence (6) are syntactically valid antecedents for the reflexive previous tests (Goodluck and Birch, 1988; Hirikawa, 1990; Eckman, 1994 and others) have often shown informants selecting the subject as the only legitimate antecedent. However, as was discussed in Section 3.3.3 there is a strong claim that this is due to a preference for the subject rather than a prohibition on non-subject antecedents.

Type 4: bi-clausal sentences with a clause containing a sub-commanding NP

(7) **Becky thought Sally's mother hated herself.**

In sentence (7) only the head of the NP, *Sally's mother* c-commands the reflexive and can, therefore, be its antecedent. However, as with Type 1 sentences, the acceptance of sentence (7) does not preclude the possibility that informants are interpreting *Sally* or *Becky* as the antecedent for the reflexive. If we compare sentence (7) to (8):

(8) **Becky thought Sally's father hated herself.**

Local binding would be prevented by the clash in features and informants' acceptances would be evidence for them permitting LD binding.

Type 5: bi-clausal sentences containing a relative clause and a reflexive in the main clause

(9) **The man who Jack saw watched himself on TV.**

In Type 5 sentences only the subject of the relative clause, *the man* is within the governing category of the reflexive. Therefore, if informants adopt a strategy[5] of interpreting reflexives as being bound to the nearest potential antecedent based upon linear order they would assign the wrong interpretation to the subject of the relative clause (*Jack*). Type 5 sentences act as controls to determine whether informants might be "giving the right interpretation for the wrong reasons" (Thomas, 1993: 76) in the case of Types 1,2 and 3. On those types it is possible for informants to appear to be making target-like judgments on the basis of allowing binding of the reflexive by the closest antecedent. If they were operating on that basis, they would choose the non-target option in the case of Type 5 sentences.

Type 6: uniclausal sentences with a reflexive inside a "picture NP" with a possessor

(10) Becky liked Sally's photographs of herself.

In sentence (10) the reflexive is bound to the possessor in the "picture NP", i.e. *Sally*. However, as was pointed out by Kuno (1987) and Reinhart and Reuland (1993) there appears to be some speaker variability and reflexives may not be restricted to taking the possessor as the antecedent. Reinhart and Reuland (1993: 683) give the following example:

(11) */? Lucie$_i$ liked your picture of herself$_i$.

and claim that, "the judgments on NP anaphora are much less clear than the linguistic literature tends to assume." (Reinhart and Reuland 1993:683). Empirical research by Keller and Asudeh (2001), Asudeh and Keller (2001) and Runner et al. (2003) offer further evidence that many native speakers will accept reflexives bound to the subject of the sentence. Runner et al. (2003) found that their informants chose the possessor as the antecedent 70-75% of the time, but the subject of the sentence 25-30% of the time. Runner and Kaiser (2005: 598) argue, "the fact that the possessor was chosen significantly less often than the 100% predicted by Binding Theory suggests that antecedent choice is not guided purely by Binding Theory."

Runner et al. (2002:402) commenting on the contrast between sentences (12) and (13) note, "structural constraints do not seem relevant since the reflexive is not even in the same sentence as its antecedent.

> **(12) John was going to get even with Mary. That picture of himself in the paper would really annoy her, as would the other stunts he had planned.**

> **(13) *Mary was taken aback by the publicity John was receiving. That picture of himself in the paper had really annoyed her, and there was not much she could do about it.**

Their analysis of this difference is based on logophoric factors. Thus, in sentence (12) the reflexive can take the extra-sentential NP as its antecedent as the discourse is from the point of view of *John*.

Type 7: uni-clausal sentence containing a reflexive

> **(14) Jack saw himself in the mirror.**

This type of sentence tests whether informants are treating reflexives as bound anaphors. By contrasting examples like sentence (14) with similar sentences containing pronominals it establishes if informants recognize and differentiate between pairs such as *him/ himself, you/ yourself* etc. In addition, it allows a check on whether gender features are recognized by testing to see if informants who accept sentences like (14) reject sentences like (15).

(15) *Jack saw herself in the mirror.

In the two English tests there were a total of 53 sentences which contained a reflexive. Figure 6.3 gives the number of sentence types used in each test.

Figure 6.5 Number of stimuli by sentence type

Sentence Type	Test 1	Test 2	Total
1	5	7	12
2	4	7	11
3	3	6	9
4	1	-	1
5	2	2	4
6	4	10	14
7	2	-	2
Totals	21	32	53

6.4 Test Descriptions

Two tests were conducted. Test 1 was a grammaticality judgment task. Test 2 was a truth-value judgment task.

6.4.1 Vocabulary

The vocabulary employed in the test was designed to be easily understood by all the informants. Appendix 3 lists all the verbs used. A total of five proper names were used. The gender was designed to be readily recognizable. However, to ensure correct recognition all tests included a picture sheet with all the proper names assigned to illustrations which were clearly either male or female. In addition, as the names of the informants were known, none of the names that were selected was identical to the names of the informants. An example is shown in Figure 6.6.

Figure 6.6 Test illustration

In addition, all other words were selected based on their relative frequency and simplicity. They were cross checked to ensure that they all appeared on the Taiwan High school index of the 500 words most frequent English words.

6.4.2 Test 1

In Test 1 informants were presented with 52 sentences; 21 sentences contained a reflexive and were, therefore, the focus of this research. The remaining 31 sentences were fillers which were designed to obscure the focus of the research. Informants were asked to judge whether the test sentences were grammatically acceptable. Informants were informed both orally and in writing that all spelling and punctuation was correct. This was done to try and reduce the possibility that sentences would be judged less acceptable due to erroneously perceived non-syntactic errors. Prior to the commencement of the test the question format was demonstrated using sentences which were not relevant to binding research. In this test each sentence was presented with informants being asked to select *"OK"* if the sentence was a legitimate English sentence and *"Not OK"* if it was not. An example of the question format is shown in Figure 6.7.

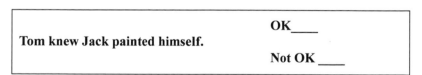

| **Tom knew Jack painted himself.** | **OK**____ |
| | **Not OK** ____ |

Figure 6.7 Test 1: question format

As English reflexives are syntactically marked, the antecedent and the reflexive must agree with respect to these features. This contrast can be seen in the following two sentences:

(16) **Jack drew himself.**
(17) ***Sally drew himself.**

131

In the sentence in Figure 6.7 the local NP, *Jack* and the reflexive *himself* are both marked as [male, 3rd person singular]. In addition, all the grammatical requirements[6] are met for an antecedent and as this sentence is presented without any context the expected response is that this sentence is *OK*. However, there is the possibility that an acceptance is based on LD binding as informants could be interpreting the subject of the higher clause, *Tom* as the antecedent of the reflexive as it also marked as [male, 3rd person singular]. If we contrast this sentence with:

(18) Sally knew Jack hated herself.

The contrast in features between *Jack* and the reflexive *herself* precludes binding. Binding of the reflexive to *Sally* would be prohibited in our model for two reasons. First, an X^{max} reflexive is prohibited from moving out of its original clause. In addition, even if it is erroneously analysed as an X^o reflexive, when it adjoins to I there will be a contrast in features and it cannot be interpreted. Furthermore, if the reflexive did not carry features in the ILG of an informant the assignment of features when it adjoins to I would mean that these features would percolate up from Spec I. As the subject of the higher clause differs in gender features from the subject of the lower clause, it would be blocked. Thus, an acceptance of this sentence would not seem to agree with the head-movement at LF model proposed in this study.

6.4.3 Test 2

Test 2 comprised 35 sentences. Thirty two sentences contained a reflexive and the other three sentences contained only R-expressions. No filler sentences were used due to the timing constraints. The informants were presented with an answer sheet with a choice between "true" and "false" for each question. The answer sheet did not contain either the written or pictorial stimuli.

In addition to the illustrations for the proper names (see Figure 6.1), an illustration of the test administrator was included along with a stick figure illustration corresponding to the informant ("you"). This was to ensure that informants did not give confused answers based on differing interpretations of the first and second person pronouns. This is shown in Figure 6.8.

Figure 6.8 Test 2: illustrations for first and second person pronouns.

Figure 6.9 Test 2: example illustration

Test 2 was a truth-value judgment task based upon a context provided by illustrations. All the illustrations featured either two or three characters. The informants were given an initial training session in order to ensure that the intended interpretation of the pictures was understood by the informants. Informants were shown a series of pictures like Figure 6.9.

It was then explained that the character shown at the top of the picture, in this example *Tom*, is interacting with the entire scene and is, therefore, the subject and the bottom half of the picture is the predicate. Likewise the character shown in the left corner, i.e. *Jack*, is interacting with the TV. Thus, sentences such as "Tom saw Jack watching TV" or "Jack watched TV" etc. would be consistent with the picture and therefore true. However, "Tom was watching TV" or "Jack thinks Tom watched TV", though grammatical English sentences, would be false as they do not describe the visual stimulus. Furthermore, sentences, such as "Tom see Jack watch TV" would also be false as though it can be interpreted to be consistent with the picture it is ungrammatical. Therefore, informants were effectively being asked to make judgments based on both grammar and meaning. In this training no pronominals or reflexives were employed. In addition, the test included three questions where all the NPs were r-expressions. These questions were designed to ensure informants were interpreting the visual stimuli in the "correct" way, so the data from any respondents who misinterpreted them could be excluded.

In the test, informants were shown a picture which was projected onto a screen. After a pause of three seconds an accompanying sentence was revealed beneath the image. Each informant then recorded his or her answer of either "true" or "false" on the answer sheet. The image was then replaced with the next image in the test. Therefore, informants did not have the opportunity to refer to previous test stimuli when they were completing the test.

6.4.4 Testing Procedures

The main subject pool was drawn from undergraduate students at Shih Chien University in Taiwan who had participated in the Mandarin Tests described in Chapter 5. As with the Mandarin studies participation was voluntary and all participants were entered into a lottery with 12 prizes, each valued at about £10. In order to try and avoid potential data skewing due to any question order effects the subjects were split into four groups, with each group having a different randomly selected question order for each of the two tests.[7]

The tests were run in two separate sessions approximately three months apart.[8] Test 1 preceded Test 2. Prior to both tests informants were given written and oral instructions in English. In Test 1 informants were asked to complete the test, give it to the test administrator and then leave the room. They were given up to 35 minutes to complete Test 1. However, most informants completed the test in 20 to 25 minutes. In Test 2 after the initial training on the pictures, described in section 6.5.3, and the instructions the actual test sessions lasted approximately 20 minutes.

6.5 Results

Figures 6.10 to 6.14 report the responses given by each of the three groups: Mandarin speaking low level English learners, Mandarin speaking high level English learners, and native-speaking controls. The results are given in percentages and they show the acceptance rates for the indicated sentence type.

135

6.5.1 Results of Test 1

Figure 6.11 shows the results for Test 1, by sentence type, for sentences where there was a potential local antecedent with features that matched the features of the reflexive. The sentence types were as follows:

Type 1: Multi-clausal sentences with the reflexive in a subordinate tensed clause.

Type 2: Bi-clausal sentences with a non-tensed subordinate clause containing areflexive.

Type 3: Uni-clausal sentences with subject and non-subject NPs.

Type 4: Biclausal sentences with a clause containing a sub-commanding NP.

Type 5: Bi-clausal sentences containing a relative clause and a reflexive in the mainclause.

Type 6: Uniclausal sentences with a reflexive inside a "picture NP" with a possessor.

Type 7: Uniclausal sentence containing a reflexive.

Thus, these nine stimuli are those that are "correct" in that all requirements for binding are satisfied.[9] Thus, it would be anticipated that they would be rated as "OK" by informants whose grammars were consistent with the grammar of English. ANOVA testing was performed and a significant difference was found between groups: $F(2,82) = 8.62$, $p<0.01$. Post hoc Scheffé tests showed the only significant difference ($p<0.01$) was between the low learner group and the control group.

If we look at these results it seems that the responses of the informants (and the native-speaking controls) are largely consistent with them having grammars which are not inconsistent with the grammar of English. Thus the high rates of acceptance across sentence types by both the high and low learner groups suggest that the informants are largely binding reflexives to the correct local antecedent.

Figure 6.10 Test 1: showing % of sentences judged as grammaticallyacceptable for stimuli containing a local antecedent.

Senten ce Type	Tokens	L1 Mandarin				N.S. Control MeanRange %%	
		Low MeanRange %%		High MeanRange %%			
Type 1	2	88.6	85.7-91.4	86.6	82.9-91.4	97.7	93.3-100
Type 2	1	71.4		85.7		93.3	
Type 3							
Subject	1	97.1		97.1		100	
Object	2	58.6	54.3-62.9	70.0	65.7-74.3	90.0	86.7-93.3
Type 5	1	85.7		88.6		100	
Type 6	1	77.1		94.3		100	
Type 7	1	97.1		94.3		100	
Total	9	80.3	54.3-97.1	86.0	65.7- 97.1	96.3	86.7-100

Figure 6.11 shows the results for sentences where there was no candidate antecedent which could legitimately be bound to the reflexive. In these sentences all NPs whose features agreed with the reflexive were not in the local domain. Thus, these sentences were ungrammatical.

The results shown in Figure 6.11 are again consistent with the informants largely operating with grammars consistent with English grammar. ANOVA testing revealed a significant difference between the groups: $F(2,82) = 6.64$, $p<0.05$. Post hoc Scheffé tests again showed that the only significant difference ($p<0.05$) was between the low learner and the control groups.

Figure 6.11

Test 1: showing % of sentences judged as grammaticallyacceptable
for stimuli not containing a grammatical local antecedent

Sentence Type	Tokens	L1 Mandarin				N.S. Control Mean Range %%	
		Low Mean Range %%		High Mean Range %%			
Type 1	3	7.6	2.9-11.4	6.7	2.9-8.6	2.2	0-6.7
Type 2	3	16.2	14.3-17.1	11.4	8.6-14.3	0	
Type 4	1	8.6		14.3		0	
Type 5	1	11.4		2.9		0	
Type 6	3	31.5	22.9-42.9	28.6	22.9-40	26.7	6.7-40.0
Type 7	1	0		2.9		0	
Total	12		2.9-42.9				

6.5.2 Results by Sentence Type

6.5.2.1 Type 1 Sentences.

All groups showed high levels of local and low levels of LD
binding. There were no significant differences in the rates of
acceptance of tensed biclausal sentences when the candidate NP was
local or long distance.

6.5.2.2 Type 2 Sentences.

ANOVA testing showed a significant group difference: $F(2,82) =$
4.06, $p<0.05$. Post hoc Scheffé tests showed that the only significant

difference (p<0.05) was between the low learner and the control groups.

6.5.2.3 Type 3 Sentences.

In common with earlier studies there was a greater willingness to accept subject rather than object antecedents. This asymmetry was shown by all three groupsAs was discussed in Section 3.3.3, previous studies have had problems with under reporting due to preference judgments, particularly with regard to object antecedents. Though it would be premature to claim that this study totally overcomes this, the fact that between 54.7 and 74.0 % of object antecedents were deemed acceptable could indicate that this study is, compared to most previous studies, capturing insights on what is "acceptable" rather than what is "preferred".

6.5.2.4 Type 4 Sentences.

The majority of respondents in all groups rejected sentences where a sub-commanding NP was the candidate antecedent for the reflexive. There were no significant differences between the groups.

6.5.2.5 Type 5 Sentences.

In sentences where the candidate NP was structurally local, but not the closest in linear order, acceptance rates were 86% for the low learner group and 89% for the high learner group. The corresponding rates for when the candidate NP was the linearly (but not structurally) closest were 11% (low learner group) and 3% (high learner group). Therefore, it appears that there is little evidence that informants were using a "non-structural closest NP" strategy in interpreting reflexives.

6.5.2.6 Type 6 Sentences.

All groups reported high rates of acceptance when the candidate NP was the local possessor. Interestingly, when the candidate NP was the subject of the sentence the rates of acceptance were also relatively high: 32% for the low learner group, 29% for the high learner group, and 27% for the control group.

6.5.2.7 Type 7 Sentences.

The acceptance rates for uniclausal sentences containing a candidate NP and a reflexive with the same features were above 94% for all groups. Thus, these results seem to provide evidence that informants readily accept local binding. The rates for Type 1 sentences, where the features of the NP and the reflexive did not agree, were 3% for the low learner group and 7 % for the high learner group. Thus, there was evidence that the informants were aware of the gender features of English reflexives (and the gender features of the r-expressions employed in these tests). In addition, it is also evidence that informants' grammars require an antecedent for a reflexive as an unspecified extra-sentential antecedent did not seem to be a legitimate option.[10]

6.5.3 Results for Test 2

In common with Test 1, the greatest acceptance of the non local antecedents was in Type 6 sentences. However, there was no significant difference between the learner groups and the native-speaking controls.

Figure 6.12 Test 2: showing % of sentences accepted
when the indicated antecedent is a local subject.

Sentence Type	Tokens	L1 Mandarin				N.S. Control Mean Range %%	
		Low Mean Range %%		High Mean Range %%			
Type 1	3	89.5	82.9-94.3	92.4	88.6-94.3	97.8	93.3-100
Type 2	3	76.2	68.6-80.0	84.8	77.1-91.4	100	
Type3	3	96.2	91.4-100	95.2	91.4-97.1	100	
Type 5	1	94.3		91.4		100	
Type 6	3	77.1	71.4-82.9	90.5	85.7-97.1	88.9	86.7- 93.3
Total	13	85.5	68.6-100	90.8	77.1-97.1	96.9	86.7-100

Figure 6.12 shows the results from Test 2 where the NP bound to the reflexive illustrated in the stimulus was local, and thus grammatically legitimate. The results indicate most informants rated such stimuli as "correct". Therefore, it was largely in line with the results from Test 1. ANOVA tests detected a significant difference: $F(2,82) = 3.41$, $p<0.05$. Post hoc Scheffé tests showed a significant difference between the low learner group and the native controls. This was also similar to the results from Test 1, where no significant difference was detected either between the two learner groups or between the high learner group and the control group.

Figure 6.13 shows the acceptance rate for when the indicated antecedent was an object. The results again consistently show rates in excess of 50% acceptance. This also reflects the results from Test 1 as does the fact that the rates of acceptability where less than for subjects in such uniclausal sentences. There were significant differences between subjects and objects for all three groups.[10]

Figure 6.13 Test 2: showing % of sentences accepted
when the indicated antecedent is a local non-subject.

Sentence Type	Tokens	L1 Mandarin				N.S. Control Mean Range %%	
		Low Mean Range %%		High Mean Range %%			
Type3	3	70.5	65.7-77.1	65.7	57.1-74.3	91.1	88.8-93.3

Figure 6.14 reports the results for sentences where the contexts provided by the visual stimuli indicate that the reflexive is bound to a non-local NP. Therefore, the interpretation of such sentences as "true" would be problematic as it would indicate the acceptance of long-distance binding. However, in a de-contextualized environment six of the sentences would be grammatical in that the local NP could be the antecedent, whereas in the other nine sentences local binding was not available as the features of the reflexive and the local NP did not agree. This could therefore be a cause of confusion in the test and consequently in the data that ensues as informants could erroneously judge the six "grammatical" sentences because they are interpretable. However, no significant differences were discovered.

The results show that non local antecedents were less acceptable than local ones. However, the rates of acceptance were consistently higher than for similar sentences in Test 1. The tendency for Type 6 sentences to be more readily accepted was also apparent. There were no significant differences between the groups. However, when we examine long distance candidate antecedents we find significant differences ($p<0.05$) as to whether they are accepted depending upon whether they are 1st/ 2nd person or 3rd person for all groups. Thus, if the indicated non-local NP is 1st or 2nd person informants judge it more acceptable than a 3rd person NP.

Finally, when the individual performances of individuals were examined in the L1 and L2 no significant correlations were found.

Figure 6.14 Test 2: showing % of sentences accepted
when the indicated antecedent is a LD subject.

Sentence Type	Candidate NP	L1 Mandarin				N.S. Control Mean.Range %%	
		Low Mean.Range %%		High Mean.Range %%			
Type 1 3rd	3	22.9	20-25.7	27.6	20.0-34.3	11.1	0-13.3
1st/2nd	1	37.1		37.1		13.3	
Type 2 3rd	3	27.6	17.1-37.1	21.9	17.1-31.4	2.2	0-6.7
1st/2nd	1	42.9		45.7		33.3	
Type 6 3rd	4	45.7	28.6-57.1	47.1	42.9-51.4	35.0	20.0-46.7
1st/2nd	3	66.7	60.0-74.3	58.1	57.1- 60.0	62.2	53.3-66.7
Totals 3rd	10	40.7	22.9-57.1	40.0	31.4-57.1	25.0	0-53.3
1st/2nd	5	53.6	37.1-74.3	48.6	37.1-57.1	40.0	13.3-66.7

6.6 Summary

Results from these tests lead to the following conclusions about learners" interpretations about reflexives in English. First, it seems that there is strong evidence that learners treat English reflexives as locally bound anaphors. The majority of respondents bind reflexives in tensed clauses to the local antecedent. High acceptance rates for sentences containing a valid local antecedent was shown in both Type 1 (multi-clausal sentences with the reflexive in a subordinate tensed clause) and Type 7 (uniclausal sentence containing a reflexive) sentences. Likewise, long-distance antecedents were largely unacceptable in such sentences. Furthermore, the data from sentences containing a relative clause show acceptance of the structurally local antecedent. This would be consistent with learners having instantiated the settings of English into their ILGs. However, caution must be exercised as it is possible to argue that this could be due to the transfer of the L1 setting for the polymorphemic reflexive *taziji*. However, the rather unclear data emerging from the Mandarin tests suggest that it is problematic to assume that *taziji* behaves as a polymorphemic reflexive which must be locally bound.

The acceptability of local binding of reflexives to subjects is again demonstrated in Type 3 uniclausal sentences. The data for the object in such sentences is less conclusive. although the majority of responses did allow such antecedents. However it would be hard to maintain that this is conclusive evidence that informants" ILGs disallow this. The repeated evidence from other empirical studies that the subject is often the preferred antecedent would seem to corroborate the data in this study.

The data from Type 2 (bi-clausal sentences with a non-tensed subordinate clause containing a reflexive) sentences, where the reflexive was contained in an untensed subordinate clause largely show that local binding is again acceptable and that long-distance binding is not. However, it is interesting to note that both the English learner groups and the native-speaking controls showed a greater tendency to accept long-distance first or second person antecedents.

The responses of informants to Type 6 (uniclausal sentences with a reflexive inside a "picture NP" with a possessor) sentences which contain a reflexive in a NP with a possessor provide some of the most interesting data. The results for acceptance of the local subject are broadly consistent with the data from the other sentence types. The results from the non-local subject of the sentence are not, in that informants are far more likely to accept such sentences.

6.7 Conclusions

In this section the place of UG in SLA will be discussed. However, as a purely syntactic model does not seem to offer explanatory adequacy, the next chapter will outline a model which combines syntactic and semantic elements to best account for the data from this study.

The data from these experiments support the idea that the behaviour of reflexives in the informants ILGs are constrained by UG. There was no evidence from Type 5 sentences (bi-clausal sentences containing a relative clause and a reflexive in the main clause) that informants were using a non-linguistic strategy of choosing the closest antecedent in linear order. In addition, the data showed that learners' ILGs largely showed that reflexives were bound in their governing categories. The data from the Mandarin tests showed that monomorphemic reflexives could be bound long-distance. However, there was little evidence of long-distance binding for English polymorphemic reflexives. This is especially marked in sentence Type 1(multi-clausal sentences with the reflexive in a subordinate tensed clause) and Type 2 (bi-clausal sentences with a non-tensed subordinate clause containing areflexive). It would seem that it is unlikely that this could be explained by general learning mechanisms due to its abstract nature. Thus, if we examine sentences with a tensed clause and the sentences containing relative clauses a reasonable interpretation would be that both learners and native speakers treat reflexives in accordance with the expected theoretical view. This would, therefore, be evidence that both groups are operating with UG-constrained grammars.

This argument could also be extended to be the case with Type 3 (uni-clausal sentences with subject and non-subject NPs) sentences, where lower rates of acceptance of non-subject antecedents has been found repeatedly in other studies. Thus, if we accept the arguments (see Section 3.3.3) of Thomas (1993), White et al. (1997), Akiyama (2002) and others and accept that the non-acceptance of local non-subject antecedents is due to "preference" rather than showing the true nature of the underlying grammar then the data is consistent with polymorphemic reflexives not only being subject orientated.

However, the data is less clear on the question of what kind of access do L2 learners have to UG. A major reason for this is the uncertainty about *taziji*. This research did not specifically set out to analyse the status of *taziji* in the grammars of native-Mandarin speakers. Therefore, practical considerations of test design led to the number and variety of test stimuli being limited. This means that any conclusions drawn about the status of *taziji* have to be tentative.

If we were to assume that *taziji* is considered a polymorphemic reflexive in the grammars of Mandarin speakers then it would seem that L1 transfer could account for the data from the English tests. However, it is not clear whether we can make this claim as the status of *taziji* in the grammars of the informants did not seem to be universally that certain. As some informants preferred the long-distance antecedent for *taziji* and/ or rated such antecedents as grammatical there are problems in categorically maintaining that the L1 settings for polymorphemic reflexives fully explain the behaviour in the L2. Indeed the argument could be made that, if the data shows that informants accept LD binding for *taziji*, there is no evidence that a locally-bound X^{max} reflexive is present in their L1. Thus, this would apparently be evidence for the full availability of UG in the L2.

However, this conclusion would be premature. As Packard (2000) and others have pointed out the complexity in establishing a word in Mandarin would not preclude an analysis that the data is showing two analyses. Thus, when long distance binding is selected the pronominal *ta* is being analysed as a separate word and as a pronominal it is free in its governing category. However, when *taziji* is interpreted as a single word it is treated as a polymorphemic reflexive.

Type 6 (uniclausal sentences with a reflexive inside a "picture NP" with a possessor) sentences also show that the local antecedent is readily accepted and is, therefore, consistent with learners' having access to the instantiation of UG found in English. However, the marked increase in acceptance of the sentential subject is problematic for a syntactic account. This problem is not constrained to L2 learners, but is also shown by the native speakers. Thus, it would be difficult to argue that the data from L2 learners is indicating a non UG sanctioned grammar if data from native speakers is similar. These issues, concerning Type 6 sentences, will be addressed in the next chapter.

Notes

1. Three informants only completed Test 1; three informants failed to complete all the answers; and two informants answers on the control questions in Test 2 were not consistent with the intended meanings of the pictorial stimuli.
2. No significant difference was found.
3. The informants' scores ranged from 24 to 44. This meant that 43 of the informants were classified as intermediate and 27 as lower intermediate.
4. See Chapter 3, footnote 16.
5. Such a strategy could be seen as evidence of non-linguistic problem solving.
6. i.e. Principle A, c-command and governing category.
7. See chapter 5, footnote 3.
8. Due to practical considerations the native-speaking controls were tested in single sessions.
9. i.e. Principle A, c-command and governing category.
10. This conclusion is supported by the much higher rates of acceptance of sentences in the test which contained unspecified pronouns.

· Chapter 7 ·

A Combined Semantic
and Syntactic Model of Binding

7.1 Introduction

In this chapter a model of reflexive binding will be discussed. It will be argued that a purely syntactic account does not offer an adequate explanatory framework. In order to explain the responses recorded in the tests used in this study a semantic element must also be included. The model presented will posit that NPs which could be potential antecedents are constrained by syntax, but these syntactic rules can be broken if semantic factors lead to an interpretation that is "non-syntactic". Furthermore, the strength of these semantic factors varies and, therefore, the acceptability, and hence the grammaticality, of non-syntactically bound antecedents is a variable quality. This means that the interpretation of antecedents as either grammatical or not grammatical is not always a clear dichotomy.

7.2 A combined Syntactic and Semantic model

The data from the Mandarin tests (see chapter 5) show an asymmetry between third person and first or second person antecedents.

This it was argued was due to the first or second person pronouns being the centre of deixis and, therefore, being logophorically favoured. In these tests, first or second person antecedents were deemed more acceptable than third person ones when they were in a syntactically "illicit" position. This interpretation led to a model where binding has both syntactic and non-syntactic components. Cole, Hermon and Lee (2001) argued that Mandarin reflexives had to satisfy both logophoric and syntactic requirements. When both of these requirements are met by a potential antecedent then its interpretation is completely felicitous. However, if either syntactic or logophoric factors meant that an NP was not favoured as the antecedent of a reflexive its felicity was reduced.

The data from English also seems to show non-syntactic factors being a component of the binding pattern of reflexives. If we return to the arguments of Reuland and Sigurjonsdottir (1997) (see Section 2.6.3 :49-51) we have syntactic and semantic modular components of binding. They argue that the syntactic component is preferred with the semantic component becoming available only when a syntactic interpretation is unavailable. The model presented here is that there is a syntactic and semantic interpretation of reflexives, syntactic as in the head-movement account and semantic as in logophoric. However, the clear hierarchy of syntactic interpretation having to be unavailable before the semantic component can be employed does not appear to be supported by the data. Rather it appears that these two modules seem to be both employed when a sentence is interpreted. If the syntax and semantics both lead to the same interpretation then there is no conflict and the interpretation is straightforward and in accordance with the syntactic model. However, if logophoric factors indicate an NP antecedent which is not available according to the syntactic model then this interpretation seems to become increasingly available depending upon the strength of the semantic factors.

In research into the acquisition of reflexives in children a number of researchers have noted that children have more difficulty in interpreting reflexives that are logophorically bound than those that are syntactically bound. Chien et al. (1993) found that Mandarin speaking children in Taiwan had difficulty with using ziji as a LD reflexive. Avrutin (1999) and Avrutin et al (2003) found that Dutch speaking children had very early command of the syntactic principles of their language. Hestvik and Philip (2001) studying the acquisition of Norwegian divide binding into "core binding" which is syntactic and non-core which is logophoric.

This division of binding into two distinct areas would then be consistent with the theory that a reflexive is constrained by the head-movement account. X^{max} reflexives would be locally bound and X^0 reflexives can move from I to I into a higher clause. Thus, the syntactic relation between a reflexive and its antecedent is effectively local when it is syntactically bound. However, if a reflexive cannot move into a local relation with an antecedent then the sentence is either ungrammatical and cannot be interpreted or it is interpreted logophorically.

Thus, it can be argued that the variations in the data between sentence types, in the English tests (see Chapter 6), and between first/ second person and third person pronouns is based on logophoric binding. More specifically it seems that if an NP is the deitic or perspective centre of a sentence, and hence the PIVOT, then it is semantically more "prominent" as a potential antecedent. If we examine sentences where there is no potential antecedent that can be syntactically bound like sentence (1):

(1) I have never felt so angry. That disgraceful story about myself in the paper was a series of half-truths, omissions and outright lies.

there is no other NP which can be bound to the reflexive apart from the extra-sentential first person pronoun in the first sentence. Thus, there is no potential antecedent which can be syntactically bound to the reflexive and the logophoric binding of the reflexive to *I* seems to be, for at least many native-speaker, felicitous.[1] However, if we examine the following six sentences where there are local syntactically bound NPs:

(2) **Sally knew I painted myself/ herself.**

(3) **I knew Sally painted myself/ herself.**

(4) **Sally wanted me to help myself/ herself.**

(5) **I wanted Sally to help myself/ herself.**

(6) **Sally liked my picture of myself/ herself.**

(7) **I liked Sally's picture of myself. / herself**

We find that the data from the test showed that the local NP was always acceptable (assuming the φ-features of the reflexive and its antecedent matched) However, the acceptability of the non-local antecedent increased from sentences which contained an embedded finite clause (sentences (2) and (3)) to sentences which had an embedded non-finite clause (sentences (4) and (5)) to uniclausal sentences with a reflexive inside a picture NP (sentences (6) and (7). In addition, sentences with first or second person non-local NPs (sentences (3), (5) and (7)) were more acceptable than those with third person non-local NPs (sentences (2), (4) and (6)).

This variation in the acceptability of a non-local NP as an antecedent of the reflexive seems to be due to a variation in the "semantic prominence" of these NPs based on a series of different criteria. First is the context in which the sentence appears. In the Mandarin Tests and the English Test 1, all sentences were presented without context. However in the English Test 2 the illustrations provided a context which deitically indicated the non-local NP. Second, is that sentences like (2) and (3) contain an embedded sentence. Therefore, the reflexive has a local sentential subject which is the centre of perspective of that (embedded) sentence. However, the sentential subject of the other sentences is the non-local NP. Finally, if we examine sentences like (6) and (7) the arguments of the verb are the sentential subject and the NP with the head, picture.[2] Therefore the possessor contained within the "picture" NP is not a direct argument of a verb. Thus, there are not two arguments of the verb "competing" as candidate antecedents for the reflexive.

This would mean we have a scale of semantic prominence which would place *Sally* from sentence (2) as the least prominent and *I* from sentence (7) as the most prominent. Thus, in sentence (2) there is an embedded sentential subject, two NPs which are arguments of the matrix verb and the non-local antecedent is third person. However, in sentence (7) the non-local NP is the only sentential subject, the sole NP argument of a verb which can act as an antecedent and a first person pronoun. The semantic prominence and, therefore, the acceptability of the long-distance NPs in sentences (3) to (6) will be at intermediate values on this scale. Figure 7.1 shows the breakdown of sentences and whether the non-local NP is semantically indicated by the three criteria discussed above.

Figure 7.1 Semantic factors favouring a LD antecedent by sentence type.

Sentence	No embedded sentence	no "competing" argument	first/second person
2. Sally knew I painted myself/ herself.	×	×	×
3. I knew Sally painted myself/ herself.	×	×	√
4. Sally wanted me to help myself/ herself.	√	×	×
5. I wanted Sally to help myself/ herself.	√	×	√
6. Sally liked my picture of myself/ herself.	√	√	×
7. I liked Sally's picture of myself. / herself.	√	√	√

Therefore, the hypothesis would be that in sentences to (2) to (7) the local NP would be syntactically licensed as being bound to the reflexive; whereas, the non-local antecedents would not be syntactically licensed. However, as the semantic prominence of the non-local NP increases then the propensity for both native and non-native speakers to accept such NPs as valid antecedents for the reflexive increases. This acceptance of non-local NPs is present not only when discordant features preclude syntactic binding, like in sentence (8), but also when syntactic binding is possible, as in sentence (9).

Therefore, this study offers an explanation of reflexive binding in terms of a model whichcombines syntactic and logophoric components. This model seems to account for the data in both L1 and L2.

(8) **Jack liked Sally's picture of himself.**

(9) **Becky liked Sally's picture of herself.**

In sentence (9) the syntactically bound anaphor is *Becky,* but the semantically prominent and, therefore the "semantically licensed" anaphor is *Sally*. Therefore, in the grammars of many informants both are interpreted as valid antecedents.

Therefore, this study offers an explanation of reflexive binding in terms of a model which combines syntactic and semantic components. This model seems to account for the data in both L1 and L2.

Notes

1. See Zribi-Hertz (1989) and Baker (1995) for discussion of English reflexives which are not syntactically bound to their antecedent. See Huang (2000)for a comprehensive survey of examples from other languages.

2. See Reinhart and Reuland (1993) and Pollard and Sag (1994) for a proposal that a reflexives must be bound by a dominating coargument of the predicate that selects for it. As the possessor of a "picture NP" is not required by the head it is not an argument of the head. Keller and Asudeh (2001: 488)) claim that this "would account for the full acceptability of anaphors in PNPs." However, the data from this study would seem to cast doubt on whether there is "full acceptability".

Second language acquisition of English reflexives
by Taiwanese speakers of Mandarin Chinese

· Chapter 8 ·

Concluding Remarks

This study examined the SLA of English reflexives by native-speakers of Mandarin Chinese. The research used the head-movement at LF model developed by Cole and others. However, due to the fact that this, or any other purely syntactic, model fails to fully account for the data in the research literature the notion of logophoricity was incorporated into a "working model".

The informants' intuitions about the behaviour of reflexives in their L1 were empirically tested in order to be able to make valid claims about their extant grammars. The informants were then tested in their L2, English.

In chapter 1 four hypotheses were discussed as to the role of UG in SLA. They can be summarized as:

(1) UG is unavailable
(2) UG is fully available as in the L1
(3) UG is fully available, but there is a difference between L1 andL2 acquisition
(4) UG is partially available

The results from the empirical tests showed that learners seemed to be operating with UG-constrained grammars. The informants' ILGs appeared to be governed by rules and recognized grammatical categories. Thus, there was no evidence they were resorting to non-linguistic problem solving. If we accept that UG is available it is, however, more problematic to make definitive claims about whether learners have full or partial access. The fact that the status of polymorphemic reflexives in Mandarin was unclear means that it is possible that (some) informants were transferring L1 settings into the L2. However, as many informants freely allowed *taziji* to have an LD antecedent, there is no L1 data, for those particular informants, which provides evidence that a local polymorphemic reflexive is instantiated in their L1 grammars. Thus, it would be difficult to make categoric assertions that this data supports L1 transfer.

The results from this research seem to be in line with earlier work in the SLA of reflexives. As with Thomas (1991) there was evidence of structure dependency. In addition, there was a greater willingness to allow local subject, in preference to object, antecedents as was noted by Finer and Broselow (1986), Hirakawa (1990) and others. This data also offers support to the claims of Hamilton (1996 and 1998) that logophoricity is a factor in the behaviour of reflexives in an L2. However, the results also indicate that logophoricity does not offer a full explanation for the non-syntactic elements of binding.

Interestingly, the results from the L2 learners showed a hierarchy of acceptability for LD antecedents. This hierarchy was also shown by the native-speaking controls. The preference given to first and second person pronominals would be in accordance with a theory based upon logophoricity. However, logophoricity provides only a partial explanation. Therefore, in chapter 7 the notion of "semantic prominence" was introduced. It was then argued that interpretation of a reflexive in a sentence involves both syntactic and semantic elements. When these elements are in agreement then English (polymorphemic) reflexives are locally bound. However, when semantic (including logophoric) factors indicate an LD antecedent then the acceptability of such an antecedent depends upon its semantic prominence. This, it was argued, is present in both L1 and L2 grammars.

• Bibliography •

Abraham, W., W. Kosmeijer and E. Reuland (eds.) (1990). *Issues in Germanic syntax*. Berlin: Walter de Gruyter.

Adjeman, C. (1976). On the nature of interlanguage systems. *Language Learning* 26: 297-320.

Akiyama, Y. (2002) Japanese adult learners' development of the locality condition on English reflexives. *Studies in Second Language Acquisition* 24: 27-54.

Anagnostopolou, E. and M. Everaert, (1999) Toward a more complete typology of anaphoric expressions. *Linguistic Inquiry* 30: 97-119.

Asudeh, A. and F. Keller. (2001). Experimental evidence for a predication-based binding theory. *Papers from the 37th Meeting of the Chicago Linguistic Society.* Vol. 1:The Main session, 1-14. Chicago

Atkinson, M. (1992). *Children"s syntax: an introduction to principles and parameters theory.* Oxford: Blackwell.

Avrutin, S. (1999). *Development of the Syntax-Discourse Interface.* Kluwer Academic Publishers, Dordrecht.

Avrutin, S., S. Zuckerman and I. Vlasveld. (2003). Guised competence-childrens comprehension of Dutch reflexives in "guise" contexts. Paper presented at GALA "03 Utecht University.

Baker, C. L. (1995). Contrast, discourse prominence and intensification with special reference to locally free reflexives in British English. Language 71: 63-101.

Battistella, E. (1989). Chinese reflexivization: a movement to INFL approach. *Linguistics* 27: 987-1012.

Bennett, S. (1994). Interpretation of English reflexives by adolescent speakers of Serbo-Croatian. *Second Language Research* 7: 35-59.

Bennett, S. and L. Progovac. (1998). Morphological status of reflexives in second language acquisition. In S. Flynn, G. Martohardjono and W.

O'Neil (eds.) *The generative study of second language acquisition.* London: Lawrence Erlbaum Associates.

Bley-Vroman, R. (1989). What is the logical problem of foreign language learning? In S. Gass and J. Schacter (eds.) *Linguistic perspectives on second language acquisition.* (pp. 41-68).

Bock, J.K. (1990). Structure in Language: Creating form in talk. *American Psychologist* 45: 1221-36.

Borer, H. (1989). Anaphoric Agr. In O. Jaeggli and K. Safir (eds.). *The Null Subject Parameter.* Dordrecht: Kluwer..

Broselow, E. and D. Finer. (1991). Parameter setting in second language phonology and syntax. *Second Language Research* 7: 35-59.

Buring, D. (2005). *Binding Theory.* Cambridge: Cambridge University Press.

Carden, G. (1970). A note on conflicting idiolects. *Linguistic Inquiry* 1: 281-90.

Chao, Y.R. (1968). *A Grammar of Spoken Chinese.* Berkeley: University of California Press.

Chen, C., S. Tseng, C.-R. Huang and K.J. Chen. (1993). Some distributional properties of Mandarin Chinese: A study based on the Academia Sinica corpus. *Proceedings of the 1ˢᵗ PACFoCoL.* 81-95. Taipei

Chen, H.-C., & Zhou, X. (1999). Processing east Asian languages: An introduction. *Language and Cognitive Processes, 14,* 425-428.

Cheng, R. (1985). A comparison of Taiwanese, Taiwan Mandarin , and Peking Mandarin. *Language* 61: 352-377.

Chien, Y.-C., K. Wexler and H.-W. Chang. (1993). Children's development of long-distance binding in Chinese. Journal of East Asian Linguistics 2, 229-258.

Chierchia, G. (1989). Anaphora and attitudes *de se.* In R. Bartsch, J. van Benthem, and P. van Emde Boas (eds.), *Semantics and Contextual Expression. Dordrecht: Foris.*

Chomsky, N. (1959). A review of B. F. Skinner's *Verbal Behaviour. Language* 35: 26 58.

Chomsky, N. (1976). Conditions on Rules of Grammar. *Linguistic Analysis.* 2, 303 -351.

Chomsky, N. (1981). *Lectures on Government and Binding.* Dordrecht, Foris.

Chomsky, N. (1995). *The Minimalist Program.* MIT Press.

Christie, K. (1992). Universal Grammar in the second language: an experimental study of the cross-linguistic properties of reflexives in English, Chinese and Spanish. Doctoral Dissertation, University of Delaware, Newark.

Christie, K. and J.P. Lantolf. (1998). Bind me up bind me down: Reflexives in L2. . In S. Flynn, G. Martohardjono and W. O'Neil (eds.) *The generative study of second language acquisition.* London: Lawrence Erlbaum Associates.

Clahsen, H. (1982). *Sparcherwerb in der Kindheit.* Tubingen: Narr.

Clahsen, H. (1990/91). Constraints on parameter setting: a grammatical analysis of some acquisition stages in German child language. *Language Acquisition* 1: 361-91.

Clahsen, H., S. Eisenbeiss and A. Vainikka. (1994). The seeds of structure: a syntactic analysis of the acquisition of Case marking. In T. Hoekstra and B. Schwarrtz (eds.), *Language acquisition studies in generative grammar* (pp. 85-118). Amsterdam: John Benjamins.

Clahsen, H. and U. Hong. (1995). Agreement and null subjects in German L2 development: new evidence from reaction-time experiments. *Second Language Research* 11: 57-87.

Clahsen, H., J. Meisel and M. Pienemann (1983). *Deutsch als Zweitsprache. Der Spracherwerb auslandischer Arbeiter.* Tubingen: Narr.

Clahsen, H. and P. Muysken. (1986). The availability of universal grammar to adult and child learners: a study of the acquisition of German word order. *Second Language Research* 2: 93-119.

Clements, G. N. (1975). The logophoric pronoun in Ewe: its role in discourse. *Journal of West African Languages* 10: 141-77.

Cole , P., G. Hermon and L.-M. Sung. (1990). Principles and parameters of long-distance reflexives. *Linguistic Inquiry* 21: 1-21.

Cole , P. and L.-M. Sung. (1994). Head movement and long-distance reflexives. *Linguistic Inquiry* 25: 355-406.

Cole , P. and C.-C Wang. (1996). Antecedent and blockers of long distance reflexives: the case of Chinese *ziji. Linguistic Inquiry* 27: 357-90.

Cole , P., G. Hermon and C.-L. Lee. (2001). Grammatical and discourse conditions on long distance reflexives in two Chinese dialects. In P. Cole,

G. Hermon and C.-T. Huang (eds.). *Syntax and Semantics: long-distance reflexives* (pp. 1-46). Vol. 33. San Diego: Academic Press.

Cook, V. (1988). *Chomsky's Universal Grammar: an introduction.* Oxford: Blackwell.

Cook, V. (1990). Timed comprehension of binding in advanced L2 learners of English. Language Learning: 40: 557-99.

Cook, V. (1993), *Linguistics and Second Language Acquisition.* Basingstoke: Macmillan,

Cook, V. and M. Newson. (1996). *Chomsky's Universal Grammar: an introduction.* Oxford: Blackwell.

Coppieters, R. (1987). Competence differences between native and near-native speakers. *Language* 63: 544-73.

Corder, S. P. (1967). The significance of learners' errors. *International Review of Applied Linguistics 5*: 161-70.

Cowart, W. (1997). *Experimental syntax: Applying objective methods to sentence judgments.* Thousand Oaks: Sage.

Crain, S. and C. McKee. (1986). Acquisition of structural restrictions on anaphora. *Proceedings of the North Eastern Linguistic Society* 21: 1-22.

Curtis, S. (1977). *Genie: a psycholinguistic study of a modern-day "wild child'.* New York: Academic Press.

Davison, A. (1999). Lexical anaphora in Hindi-Urdu. In B. Lust, K. Wali, J. Gair and K.V. Subbararo (eds.). *Lexical Pronouns and Anaphors in some South Asian Languages: A Principled Typology.* Berlin: Mouton de Gruyter.

Demirci, M. (2000). The role of pragmatics in reflexive interpretation by Turkish learners of English. *Second Language Research* 16: 325-53.

Dittmar, N. (1981) Regen bisschen Pause geht –More on the puzzle of inference. Paper presented at the "First European-North American Workshop on Cross-Linguistic Second Language Acquisition Research". UCLA.

du Plessis, J., D. Solin, L. Travis and L. White. (1987). UG or not UG, that is the question: a reply to Clahsen and Muysken. *Second Language Research 3:* 56-75.

Eckman, F. (1994). Local and long-distance anaphora in second-language acquisition. In E. Tarone, S. Gass and A. Cohen (eds.), *Research methodology in second-language acquisition*. Hillsdale: Lawrence Erlbaum.

Epstein, S., S. Flynn and G. Martohardjono. (1996). Second language acquisition: theoretical and experimental issues in contemporary research. *Brain and Behavioral Sciences* 19: 677-758.

Epstein, S., S. Flynn and G. Martohardjono. (1998). The strong continuity hypothesis: some evidence concerning functional categories in adult L2 acquisition. In S. Flynn, G. Martohardjono and W. O'Neil (eds.) *The generative study of second language acquisition*. (pp. 61-77).

Eubank, L. (ed.) (1991) *Point Counterpoint: Universal Grammar in the second language*.

Eubank, L. (1993/94). On the transfer of parametric values in L2 development. *Language Acquisition* 3: 183-208.

Eubank, L. (1994). Optionality and the initial state in L2 development. In T. Hoekstra and B. D. Schwartz (eds.), *The generative study of second language acquisition* (pp. 369-88).

Eubank, L. (1996). Negation in early German-English interlanguage: more valueless features in the L2 initial state. *Second Language Research* 12: 73-106.

Finer, D. (1991). Binding parameters in second language acquisition. In L. Eubank (ed.), *Point Counterpoint: Universal Grammar in the second language*. Amsterdam: John Benjamins.

Finer, D. and E. Broselow (1986). Second language acquisition of reflexive binding. *NELS* 16: 154-68

Flynn, S. (1985). Principled Theories of Adult Second Language Acquisition. *Studies in Second Language Acquisition,* 7(1): 99-107.

Flynn, S. and W. O'Neil (eds.) (1988) Linguistic theory in second language acquisition. *Dordrecth: Kluwer Academic Publishers*

Flynn, S., G. Martohardjono and W. O'Neil (eds.) (1998). *The generative study of second language acquisition*. London: Lawrence Erlbaum Associates.

Frajzyngier, Z. (1993). *A Grammar of Mupun*. Berlin: Reimer.

Gass, S. and J. Schachter (eds.) (1989) *Linguistic Perspectives on Second Language Acquisition*. New York: CUP.

Giorgi, A. (1984). Toward a theory of long-distance anaphora: A GB approach. *Linguistic Review* 3: 307-59.

Goodluck, H. and B. Birch. (1988). Late-learned rules in first and second language acquisition. In, J. Pankhurst, M. Sharwood-Smith and P. van Buren (eds.), *Learnability and second languages: A book of readings.* Dordrecht: Foris.

Hamilton, R. (1996). Against underdetermined reflexive binding. *Second Language Research* 12: 420-46.

Hamilton, R. (1998). Underdetermined binding of reflexives by adult Japanese-speaking learners of English. *Second Language Research* 14: 292-320.

Hawkins, R. (2001). *Second language syntax: a generative introduction.* Oxford: Blackwell.

Hawkins, R. and Y.-H. C. Chan. (1997). The partial availability of Universal Grammar in second language acquisition: the "failed functional feature hypothesis". *Second Language Research* 13: 187-226.

Hellan, L. (1991). Containment and connectedness anaphors. In J. Koster and E. Reuland (eds.). *Long-Distance Anaphora.* New York: Cambridge University Press.

Hermon, G. (1982). Binding theory and parameter setting. *Linguistic Review* 9: 145-81.

Hestvik, A. and W. Philip. (2001) Syntactic vs. logophoric binding. In In P. Cole, G. Hermon and C.-T. Huang (eds.). *Syntax and Semantics: long-distance reflexives.* Vol. 33. San Diego: Academic Press.

Hirakawa, M. (1990). A study of the L2 acquisition of English reflexives. *Second Language Research* 6: 60-85.

Hoekstra, T. and B. D. Schwartz (eds.) (1994). *Language acquisition studies in generative grammar.* Amsterdam: John Benjamins.

Hoosian, R. (1991). *Psycholinguistic implications for linguistic relativity: a case study of Chinese.* Hillside, NJ: Lawrence Erlbaum.

Huang, C.-T. and C.-S. Liu. (2001) Logophoricity, attitudes and ziji at the interface. In P. Cole, G. Hermon and C.-T. Huang (eds.). *Syntax and Semantics: long-distance reflexives.* Vol. 33. San Diego: Academic Press.

Huang, C.-T. and C.-C. Tang. (1991). Contextual determination of anaphor/ pronominal distinction. In J. Koster and E. Reuland (eds.). *Long-Distance Anaphora.* New York: Cambridge University Press.

Huang, Y. (1994).*The Syntax and Pragmatics of Anaphora: A study with special reference to Chinese* . Cambridge: Cambridge University Press.

Huang, Y. (1997). Interpreting long distance reflexives: a neo-Grician pragmatic approach. paper presented at the LSA Workshop on Long-Distance Reflexives: Cornell University.

Huang, Y. (2000). *Anaphora: a cross-linguistic study.* New York: Oxford.

Huang, Y.-H. (1984). Chinese Reflexives. Studies in English Literature and Linguistics 10, 163-188. National Taiwan Normal University, Taipei.

Hyams, N. M. and S. Sigurjónsdóttir. (1990). The development of "long-distance anaphora": a cross-linguistic study with special reference to Icelandic. *Language Acquisition* 1: 57-93.

Jackendorf, R. (1972). Semantic Interpretation in generative grammar. Cambridge: MIT Press.

Kang, B.-M. (1998). Unbounded Reflexives. *Linguistics and Philosophy* 11: 415-56.

Keller, F. and A. Asudeh. (2001). Constraints on linguistic coreference: structural vs. fragmatic factors. *Proceedings of the 23rd Annual Conference of the Cognitive Science Society*. Mahawah, NJ: Lawrence Erlbaum.

Kornfilt, J. (1997). *Turkish*. London: Routledge.

Kuno, S. (1972). Pronomilization, reflexivization and direct discourse. *Linguistic Inquiry* 3: 161-95.

Kuno, S. (1987). *Functional Syntax: Anaphora, Discourse and Empathy.* Chicago: The University of Chicago Press.

Labov, W. (1975). Empirical foundations of linguistic theory. In R.P. Austerlitz (ed.) *The scope of American linguistics*. Lisse: Peter de Ridder.

Lakshmanan, U. and K. Teranishi. (1994). Preference versus grammaticality judgments: some methodological issues concerning the governing category parameter in second-language acquisition. In E. Tarone, S. Gass and A. Cohen (eds.), *Research methodology in second-language acquisition*. Hillsdale: Lawrence Erlbaum.

Lebeaux, D. (1983). A distributional difference between reciprocals and reflexives. *Linguistic Inquiry* 14: 723-30.

Lees R.B. and E. Kilma. (1963). Rules for English Pronominalization. Language 39: 17-28.

Lenneberg, E. (1967). *Biological foundations of Language.* New York: John Wiley.

Lewis, D. (1979). Attitudes *de dicto* and *de se. The Philosophical Review* 88: 513-43.

Li, Y. (1993). What makes long distance reflexives possible? *Journal of East Asian Linguistics* 2: 132-66.

Liceras, J. (1997). The then and now of L2 growing pains. In L. Díaz and C. Pérez (eds.), *Views on the acquisition and use of a second language* (pp. 65-85). Barcelona: Universitat Pompeu Fabra.

MacLaughlin, D. (1995). Language acquisition and the subset principle. *The Linguistic Review* 12: 143-91.

MacLaughlin, D. (1998). The acquisition of the morphosyntax of English reflexives by non-native speakers. In M.L. Beck (ed.), *Morphology and its interfaces in second language knowledge* (pp. 195-226). Amsterdam: John Benjamins.

Maling, J. (1984). Non-clause-bounded reflexives in modern Icelandic. *Linguistcs and Philosophy* 7: 211-41.

Manzini, R. M. and K. Wexler. (1987). Parameters, binding theory, and learnability. *Linguistic Inquiry* 18: 413-44.

Matsumura, M. (1994). Japanese learners' acquisition of the locality requirement of English reflexives: Evidence for retreat from overgeneralization. *Studies in Second Language Acquisition* 16: 19-42.

Meisel, J. (1991). Principles of Universal Grammar and strategies of language learning: some similarities and differences between first and second language acquisition. In L. Eubank (ed.), *Point Counterpoint: Universal Grammar in the second language.* (pp. 231-76).

Moskovsky, C. (2004). Third person effects on binding. *Linguistics* 42: 1035-48.

Newmeyer, F.J. (1998). *Language form and language function.* Cambridge MA: MIT Press.

Newmeyer, F.J. and S.H. Weinberger. (1988). The ontogenesis of the field of second language learning research. In S, Flynn and W. O'Neil (eds.), Linguistic theory in second language acquisition.

Newson, M. (1990). Dependencies in the lexical setting of parameters: A solution to the undergeneralization problem. In I.M. Roca (ed.) Logical issues in language acquisition. *Dordrecht: Foris.*

O'Grady, W. (1996). Language acquisition without Universal Grammar a proposal for L2 learning. *Second Language Research* 12: 374-97.

Packard, J. (2000). *The morphology of Chinese: a linguistic and cognitive approach.* Cambridge: Cambridge University Press.

Pan, H.-H. (1998). Closeness, prominence, and binding theory. Natural Language and Linguistic Theory 16: 771-815.

Pan, H.-H. (2001). Why the Blocking Effect? In P. Cole, G. Hermon and C.-T. Huang (eds.). *Syntax and Semantics: long-distance reflexives.* Vol. 33. San Diego: Academic Press.

Pica, P. (1984). Subject, tense and truth: towards a modular approach to binding. In J. Gueron, H.-G. Obenauer and J.-Y. Pollock (eds.), Grammatical Representation. (pp. 259-91). Dordrecht: Foris.

Pica, P. (1987).On the nature of the reflexivisation cycle. Proceedings of NELS. *17, vol. 2: 483-99. GLSA. University of Massachusetts. Amherst.*

Pinker, S. (1994). *The language instinct.* New York: William Morrow and Co.

Pollard, C. and I.A. Sag. (1992). Anaphors in English and the scope of binding theory. *Linguistic Inquiry* 23: 261-303.

Pollard, C. and I.A. Sag. (1994). Head-driven phrase structure grammar. *Chicago: University of Chicago Press.*

Pollard, C. and P. Xue. (2001). Syntactic and nonsyntactic constraints on long-distance reflexives. In P. Cole, G. Hermon and C.-T. Huang (eds.). *Syntax and Semantics: long-distance reflexives.* Vol. 33. San Diego: Academic Press.

Progovac, L. (1992). Relativized SUBJECT: long-distance reflexives without movement.

Linguistic Inquiry 23: 671-80.

Progovac, L. (1993). Long-distance reflexives: movement-to-Infl versus relativized SUBJECT. *Linguistic Inquiry* 24: 755-72.

Reinhart, T. (1983) *Anaphora and Semantic Interpetation.* London: Croom Helm.

Reinhart, T. and E. Reuland. (1993). Reflexivity. *Linguistic Inquiry* 24: 657-720.

Reuland, E. (2001). Anaphors, logophors, and binding. In P. Cole, G. Hermon and C.-T. Huang (eds.). *Syntax and Semantics: long-distance reflexives.* Vol. 33. San Diego: Academic Press.

Reuland, E. and S. Sigurjonsdottir. (1997). Long-distance "binding" in Icelandic: Syntax or discourse. In H.J. Bennis, P. Pica and J. Rooryck (eds.) Atomism and Binding. Dordrecht: Foris.

Ritchie, W. (1978), The right roof constraint in an adult-acquired language. In W. Ritchie (ed.) *Second language acquisition research: issues and implications.* (pp. 33-63). Academic Press, New York.

Runner, J., R. Sussman and M. Tanenhaus. (2002). Logophors in possessed picture noun phrases. *WCCFL 21 Proceedings,*: 401-414. Somerville, MA: Cascadilla Press.

Runner, J., R. Sussman and M. Tanenhaus. (2003). Assignment reference to reflexives and pronouns in picture noun phrases: Evidence from eye movement. Cognition *81. 1: B1-B13.*

Runner, J. and E. Kaiser. (2005). Binding in picture noun phrases: Implications for Binding Theory. Proceedings of the HPSG05 Conference. *University of Lisbon.*

Safir, K. J. (1987). Comments on Wexler and Manzini. In T. Roeper, and E. Williams (eds.), *Parameter Setting.* (pp.77-89). Dordrecht: D. Reidel.

Schwartz, B. D. (1991). Conceptual and empirical evidence: a response to Meisel. In L. Eubank (ed.), *Point Counterpoint: Universal Grammar in the second language.*

Schwartz, B. D. and R. Sprouse. (1996). L2 cognitive states and the full transfer/ full access model. *Second Language Research 12:* 40-72.

Schwartz, B. D. and A. Tomaselli. (1990). Some implications from an analysis of German word order. In W. Abraham, W. Kosmeijer and E. Reuland (eds.), *Issues in Germanic syntax.* Berlin: Walter de Gruyter.

Selinker, L. (1972). Interlanguage. *International Review of Applied Linguistics10.* 209-31.

Sells, P. (1987). Aspects of logophoricity. Linguistic Inquiry *18: 445-79.*

Tang, C.-C. J. (1985). A study of reflexives in Chinese. Master's thesis. National Taiwan Normal University.

Tang, C.-C. J. (1989). Chinese reflexives. *Natural Language and Linguistic Theory* 7: 93-121.

Thomas, M. (1989). The interpretation of English reflexive pronouns by non-native speakers. *Studies in SecondLanguage Acquisition* 11: 281-303.

Thomas, M. (1991). Universal Grammar and the interpretation of reflexives in a second language. *Language* 67: 211-39.

Thomas, M. (1993). *Knowledge of reflexives in a second language.* Amsterdam:John Benjamins.

Thomas, M. (1995). Acquisition of the Japanese reflexive zibun and movement of anaphors in Logical Form. *Second Language Research* 11: 206-34.

Thomas, M. (1998). Binding and related issues in L2 acquisition: Commentary on part III. In S. Flynn, G. Martohardjono and W. O'Neil (eds.) *The generative study of second language acquisition.* London: Lawrence Erlbaum Associates.

Tsai, C.-H. (2001). Word identification and eye movement in reading Chinese: a modeling approach. Doctoral dissertation: University of Illinois at Urbana-Champain

Tsimpli, I.-M. and A. Roussou. (1991). Parameter resetting in L2?, *UCL Working Papers in Linguistics 3*: 149-69.

Vainikka, A. (1993/94). Case in the development of English syntax. *Language Acquisition 3*: 257-325.

Vainikka, A. and M. Young-Scholten. (1994). Direct access to X'-theory: evidence from Korean and Turkish adults learning German. In T. Hoekstra and B. D. Schwartz (eds.), *Language acquisition studies in generative grammar* (pp. 265-316). Amsterdam: John Benjamins.

Vainikka, A. and M. Young-Scholten. (1996a). Gradual development of L2 phase structure. *Second Language Research* 12: 7-39.

Vainikka, A. and M. Young-Scholten. (1996b). The early stages of adult L2 syntax: additional evidence from Romance speakers. *Second Language Research* 12: 140-76.

Wakabayashi, S. (1996). The nature of interlanguage: Second language acquisition of English reflexives. *Second Language Research* 12: 266-303.

Wexler, K. and R. M. Manzini. (1987). Parameters and learnability in Binding Theory. In T. Roeper and E. Williams (eds.), *Parameter Setting.* (pp.41-76). Dordrecht: D. Reidel.

White, L. (1989). *Universal grammar and second language acquisition*. Amsterdam: John Benjamins.

White, L. (1990). Second language acquisition and universal grammar. *Studies in Second Language Acquisition* 12: 121-33.

White, L. (1996). Universal Grammar and second language acquisition: Current trends and new directions. In W. Ritchie and T. Bhatia (eds.), Handbook of Language Acquisition. New York: Academic Press.

White, L. (2003). *Second language acquisition and Universal Grammar.* Cambridge: Cambridge University Press.

White, L., J. Bruhn de Garavito, T. Kawasaki, J. Pater and P. Prévost (1997). The researcher gave the subject a test about himself: Problems of ambiguity and preference in the investigation of reflexive binding. *Language Learning* 47: 145-72.

Xu, L. (1993) The long distance binding of *ziji*. *Journal of Chinese Linguistics 21: 123-41.*

Xu, L. (1994) The antecedent of *ziji*. *Journal of Chinese Linguistics 22: 115-37.*

Yang, D.-W. (1983). The extended binding theory of anaphors. *Language Research* 19:169-192.

Yu, X,-F. W. (1992). Challenging Chinese reflexive data. *The Linguistic Review 9: 285-94.*

Yuan, B. (1994). Second language acquisition of reflexives revisited. *Language* 70: 539-45.

Yuan, B. (1998). Interpretation of binding and orientation of the Chinese reflexive *ziji* by English and Japanese speakers. *Second Language Research* 14: 324-40.

Zribi-Hertz, A. (1989). Anaphor binding and narrative point of view: English reflexive pronouns in sentence and discourse. *Language* 65: 695-727.

· Appendix 1 ·

List of sentences used in Mandarin Test 1

Type 1: Tri-clausal sentences with the reflexive in the subordinate clause.

e.g. 秀玲聽說阿芳認為黛安討厭自己。

    (1) Shiming tingshuo Wenxiang renwei Xiaoming taoyan ziji.
           Shiming hear Wenxiang think Xiaoming hate self.
           "Shiming hears Wenxiang thinks Xiaoming hates himself."

    (2) Wenxiu tingshuo ni renwei Daian taoyan ziji.
           Wenxiu hear you think Daian hate self.
           "Wenxiu hears you think Daian hates yourself/ herself."

    (3) Wo tingshuo Xiuling renwei Afang taoyan ziji.
           I hear Xiuling think Afang hate self.
           "I hear Xiuling thinks Afang hates myself / herself."

    (4) Xiuling zhidao Afang renwei ni fangqi ziji le.
           Xiuling know Afang think you give up self LE.
           "Xiuling knows Afang thinks you have given up on herself/ yourself."

(5) Xiaoming zhidao wo renwei Shiming fangqi ziji le.

Xiaoming know I think Shiming give up self LE

"Xiaoming knows I think Shiming has given up on me/ him/ himself."

(6) Daian zhidao Afang renwei ni fangqi ziji le.

Daian know Afang think you give up self LE.

"Daian knows Afang thinks you have given up on yourself / herself."

Type 2: Bi-clausal sentences with the reflexive in the subordinate clause,

e.g. 阿芳聽說黛安討厭自己。

(7) Afang tingshuo Xiuling taoyan ziji.

Afang hear Xiuling hate ziji.

"Afang hears Xiuling hates her/ herself."

Type 3: Bi-clausal sentences with a sub-commanding potential antecedent.

e.g. 美鳳認為秀玲的學生討厭自己。

(8) Xiaoyu renwei Xiuling de xuesheng taoyan ziji.

Xiaoyu think Xiuling DE student hate self.

"Xiaoyu thinks Xiuling's student hates her/ herself."

(9) Afang renwei ni de xuesheng taoyan ziji.

Afang think you DE student hate self.

"Afang thinks your student hates you/ herself.

(10) Wo renwei Xiuling de xuesheng taoyan ziji.
I think Xiuling DE student hate self.
"I think Xiuling's student hates me/ herself."

(11) Xiaoyu renwei Xiuling de xuesheng taoyan ta ziji.
Xiaoyu think Xiuling DE student hate TA self.
"Xiaoyu thinks Xiuling's student hates herself."

Type 4: Bi-clausal sentences with a verb in the matrix clause indicating the subject of that clause has no knowledge of the proposition of the embedded clause which contains the reflexive.

e.g. 秀玲不知道阿芳討厭自己。

(12) Kexin bu zhidao Afang taoyan ziji.
Kexin not know Afang hate self.
"Kexin doesn't know Afang hates herself."

(13) Ni wangji le Afang taoyan ziji.
You forget LE Afang hate self
"You have forgotten Afang hates yourself/ herself."

(14) Afang wangji le wo taoyan ziji.
Afang forget LE I hate self.
"Afang has forgotten I hate herself/ myself."

Type 5: Bi-clausal sentences with a subject and object in the subordinate clause containing the reflexive.

e.g. 秀玲認為阿芳告訴過黛安有關自己朋友的事情。

173

(15) Xiaoming renwei ni gaosu guo Shiming youguan ziji
pengyou de shiqing.
Xiaoming think you tell GUO Shiming about self friend DE
affairs.
Xiaoming thinks you told Shiming about his/ your friend's
affairs.

(16) Wenxiang renwei Aban gaosu guo ni youguan ziji pengyou
de shiqing.
Wenxiang think Aban tell GUO you about self friend DE
affairs.
"Wenxiang thinks Aban told you about his/ your friend's
affairs."

Type 6: Uni-clausal sentences with a subject and object, and containing the reflexive in a complement phrase.

e.g. 秀玲問阿芳有關自己朋友的事情。

(17) Kexin wen Afang yoguan ziji pengyou de shiqing.
Kexin ask Afang about self friend DE affairs.
"Kexin asks Afang about her friend's affairs."

(18) Daian wen wo yoguan ziji pengyou de shiqing.
Daian ask I about self friend DE affairs.
"Daian asks me about her/ my friend's affairs."

(19) Ni wen Aban youguan ziji pengyou de shiqing.
You ask Aban about self friend DE affairs.
"You ask Aban about your/ his friend's affairs."

(20) Xiuling gaosu guo Xiaoming youguan ziji de xin gongzuo.
Xiuling tell GUO Xiaoming about self DE new work.
"Xiuling told Xiaoming about his new work."

(21) Xiuling gaosu guo Kexin youguan ta ziji de xin gongzuo.
Xiuling tell GUO Kexin about TA self DE new work.
"Xiuling told Kexin about her new work."

Second language acquisition of English reflexives
by Taiwanese speakers of Mandarin Chinese

· Appendix 2 ·

List of sentences used in Mandarin Test 2

Type 1: Tri-clausal sentences with the reflexive in the subordinate clause.

e.g. 秀玲聽說阿芳認為黛安討厭自己。

(1) Zhangsan zhidao Wenxiang renwei Xiaoming taoyan ziji.
Zhangsan know Wenxiang think Xiaoming hate self.
"Zhangsan knows Wenxiang thinks Xiaoming hates himself."

(2) Xiuling tingshuo wo renwei Daian taoyan ziji.
Xiuling hear wo think Daian hate self.
"Xiuling hears I think Daian hates yourself/ herself."

(3) Ni tingshuo Xiuling renwei Afang taoyan ziji.
You hear Xiuling think Afang hate self
"You hear Xiuling thinks Afang hates myself/ herself."

(4) Kexin zhidao Afang renwei Xiuling fangqi ta ziji le.
Kexin know Afang think Xiuling give up TA self LE.
"Kexin knows Afang thinks Xiuling has given up on herself."

(5) Xiaoming zhidao Shiming renwei wo fangqi ziji le.
Xiaoming know Shiming think I give up self LE.

"Xiaoming knows Shiming thinks I have given up on myself/himself."

Type 2: Bi-clausal sentences with the reflexive in the subordinate clause,

e.g. 阿芳聽說黛安討厭自己。

(6) Afang tingshuo wo taoyan ziji.
Afang hear I hate ziji.
"Afang hears I hate herself/ myself ."

Type 3: Bi-clausal sentences with a sub-commanding potential antecedent.

e.g. 美鳳認為秀玲的學生討厭自己。

(7) Daian renwei Xiuling de xuesheng taoyan ziji.
Daian think Xiuling DE student hate self.
"Daian thinks Xiuling's student hates herself."

(8) Afang renwei ni de xuesheng taoyan ziji.
Afang think you DE student hate self.
"Afang thinks your student hates yourself/ herself."

(9) Wo renwei Xiuling de xuesheng taoyan ziji.
I think Xiuling DE student hate self.
"I think Xiuling's student hates myself/ herself."

(10) Xiaoyu renwei Xiuling de xuesheng taoyan ziji.
Xiaoyu think Xiuling DE student hate TA self.
"Xiaoyu thinks Xiuling's student hates herself."

Type 4: Bi-clausal sentences with a verb in the matrix clause indicating the subject of that clause has no knowledge of the proposition of the embedded clause which contains the reflexive.

e.g. 秀玲不知道阿芳討厭自己。

(11) Xiuling bu zhidao Afang taoyan ziji.
Xiuling not know Afang hate self.
"Xiuling doesn't know Afang hates herself."

(12) Wo wangji le Shiming taoyan ziji.
I forget LE Shiming hate self.
"I have forgotten Shiming hates myself/ himself."

(13) Afang zhidao ni fangqi ziji le.
Afang know LE you give up self LE.
"Afang knows you have given up on herself/ yourself."

Type 5: Uni-clausal sentences with a subject and object, and containing the reflexive in a complement phrase.

e.g. 秀玲問阿芳有關自己朋友的事情。

(14) Wenxiang wen Xiaoming yoguan ziji pengyou de shiqing.
Wenxiang ask Xiaoming about self friend DE affairs.
"Wenxiang asks Xiaoming about his friend's affairs."

(15) Daian wen ni yoguan ziji pengyou de shiqing.
Daian ask you about self friend DE affairs.
"Daian asks you about her/ your friend's affairs."

(17)   Wo wen Aban youguan ziji pengyou de shiqing.
       I ask Aban about self friend DE affairs.
       "I ask Aban about your/ his friend's affairs."

(18)   Aban gaosu guo Xiaoming youguan ziji de xin gongzuo.
       Aban tell GUO Xiaoming about self DE new work.
       "Aban told Xiaoming about his new work."

· Appendix 3 ·

List of verbs used in the English tests

Verbs:

ask

draw

hate

know

like

paint

photograph

see

show

tell

think

want

watch

**Second language acquisition of English reflexives
by Taiwanese speakers of Mandarin Chinese**

• Appendix 4 •

List of sentences used in English Test 1

Type 1: Multi-clausal sentences with the reflexive in a subordinate tensed clause.

(1) Tom saw Jack photographed himself.
(2) Sally thought Jack hated himself.
(3) Becky knew Tom liked herself.
(4) I thought Sally drew myself.
(5) Tom saw you photograph himself.

Type 2: Bi-clausal sentences with a non-tensed subordinate clause containing a reflexive.

(6) Becky wanted Jack to photograph herself.
(7) Jack asked Sally to draw herself.

Type 3: Uni-clausal sentences with subject and non-subject NPs.

(8) Sally wanted me to help herself.
(9) I asked Tom to photograph myself.
(10) Tom told Becky about himself.
(11) Sally asked Jack about himself.
(12) Jack asked you about yourself.

Type 4: Bi-clausal sentences with a clause containing a sub-commanding NP.

(13) Becky thought Sally's father hated herself.

Type 5: Bi-clausal sentences containing a relative clause and a reflexive in the main clause.

(14) The man who Jack saw liked himself.
(15) The man who Sally saw liked herself.

Type 6: Uniclausal sentences with a reflexive inside a "picture NP" with a possessor.

(16) Becky liked Sally's photographs of herself.
(17) Tom liked my pictures of himself.
(18) I saw Jack's photograph of myself.
(19) Jack hated Sally's picture of himself.

Type 7: Uniclausal sentence containing a reflexive.

(20) Sally saw herself.
(21) Jack saw herself.

· Appendix 5 ·

List of sentences used in English Test 2

Bold notation shows the NP which the accompanying picture stimuli indicated.

Type 1: Multi-clausal sentences with the reflexive in a subordinate tensed clause.

(1) Tom thought **Jack** saw himself on TV.

(2) You knew **Sally** watched herself on TV.

(3) Becky thought **I** watched myself on TV.

(4) **Jack** thought Tom saw himself on TV.

(5) **Sally** knew Becky painted herself.

(6) **Tom** knew I saw himself on TV.

(7) **I** thought Sally saw myself on TV.

Type 2: Bi-clausal sentences with a non-tensed subordinate clause containing a reflexive.

(8) Sally wanted **Becky** to watch herself on TV.

(9) You asked **Tom** to watch himself on TV.

(10) Jack told **you** to watch yourself on TV.

(11) **Becky** told Sally to paint herself.

(12) **Tom** asked me to watch himself on TV.

(13) **Becky** told Tom to watch herself on TV.

(14) **You** asked Sally to watch yourself on TV.

Type 3: Uni-clausal sentences with subject and non-subject NPs.

(15) Jack showed **Tom** a picture of himself.
(16) Sally showed **you** a picture of herself.
(17) You showed **Becky** a picture of yourself.
(18) **Becky** showed Sally a picture of herself.
(19) **You** showed Tom a picture of himself.
(20) **Jack** showed me a picture of myself.

Type 4: Bi-clausal sentences containing a relative clause and a reflexive in the main clause.

(21) **The man** who Jack saw watched himself on TV.
(22) The woman who **Sally** saw watched herself on TV.

Type 5: Uniclausal sentences with a reflexive inside a "picture NP" with a possessor.

(23) Becky saw **Sally's** picture of herself.
(24) I saw **Jack's** picture of himself.
(25) Tom saw **my** picture of myself.
(26) **Sally** saw Becky's picture of herself.
(27) **Tom** liked Jack's picture of himself.
(28) **Becky** saw your picture of herself.
(29) **Sally** liked Jack's picture of herself.
(30) **You** saw Sally's picture of yourself.
(31) **You** saw my picture of yourself.
(32) **Jack** saw your picture of himself.

• Appendix 6 •

Notes on the illustrations used
in English Test 2

Accompanying the sentences in test 2 a series of 35 picture stimuli were used. These stimuli contained the following characters:

Sally   Becky

Tom   Jack

I/me   you

man   woman

Three basic patterns were used:

Pattern 1: Used for when the verbs *see* or *show* refer to the subject (i.e. Tom).

Tom saw Jack$_i$ watching himself$_i$ on TV.   Tom$_i$ saw Jack watching himself$_i$ on TV.

Pattern 2: Used for when the verbs *think, know, like* or *want* refer to the subject (i.e. Tom).

Tom liked Jack's$_i$ picture of himself$_i$.

Pattern 3: Used for when the verbs *ask* or *tell* refer to the subject (i.e. Tom).

Tom asked Jack$_i$ to paint himself$_i$.

Second language acquisition of English reflexives
by Taiwanese speakers of Mandarin Chinese

實踐大學數位出版合作系列
語言文學類　AG0114

Second language acquisition of English reflexives by Taiwanese speakers of Mandarin Chinese

作　　者	Guy Matthews
統籌策劃	葉立誠
文字編輯	王雯珊
視覺設計	賴怡勳
執行編輯	林泰宏
圖文排版	鄭維心
數位轉譯	徐真玉　沈裕閔
圖書銷售	林怡君
法律顧問	毛國樑　律師
發 行 人	宋政坤
出版印製	秀威資訊科技股份有限公司
	台北市內湖區瑞光路583巷25號1樓
	電話：(02) 2657-9211
	傳真：(02) 2657-9106
	E-mail：service@showwe.com.tw
經 銷 商	紅螞蟻圖書有限公司
	台北市內湖區舊宗路二段121巷28、32號4樓
	電話：(02) 2795-3656
	傳真：(02) 2795-4100
	http://www.e-redant.com

2009 年 7月
BOD 一版
定價：240元

讀　者　回　函　卡

感謝您購買本書，為提升服務品質，煩請填寫以下問卷，收到您的寶貴意見後，我們會仔細收藏記錄並回贈紀念品，謝謝！

1.您購買的書名：＿＿＿＿＿＿＿＿＿＿＿＿＿＿＿＿＿＿＿＿＿

2.您從何得知本書的消息？

　□網路書店　□部落格　□資料庫搜尋　□書訊　□電子報　□書店

　□平面媒體　□ 朋友推薦　□網站推薦 □其他＿＿＿＿＿＿

3.您對本書的評價：(請填代號　1.非常滿意 2.滿意 3.尚可 4.再改進)

　封面設計＿＿　版面編排＿＿　內容＿＿　文/譯筆＿＿　價格＿＿

4.讀完書後您覺得：

　□很有收獲　□有收獲　□收獲不多　□沒收獲

5.您會推薦本書給朋友嗎？

　□會　□不會，為什麼？＿＿＿＿＿＿＿＿＿＿＿＿＿＿＿＿

6.其他寶貴的意見：＿＿＿＿＿＿＿＿＿＿＿＿＿＿＿＿＿＿＿

＿＿＿＿＿＿＿＿＿＿＿＿＿＿＿＿＿＿＿＿＿＿＿＿＿＿＿＿

＿＿＿＿＿＿＿＿＿＿＿＿＿＿＿＿＿＿＿＿＿＿＿＿＿＿＿＿

＿＿＿＿＿＿＿＿＿＿＿＿＿＿＿＿＿＿＿＿＿＿＿＿＿＿＿＿

讀者基本資料

姓名：＿＿＿＿＿＿＿＿＿＿　年齡：＿＿＿＿　性別：□女 □男

聯絡電話：＿＿＿＿＿＿＿＿　E-mail：＿＿＿＿＿＿＿＿＿＿

地址：＿＿＿＿＿＿＿＿＿＿＿＿＿＿＿＿＿＿＿＿＿＿＿＿＿

學歷：□高中(含)以下　　□高中　□專科學校　　□大學

　　　□研究所(含)以上 □其他＿＿＿＿＿＿＿＿

職業：□製造業 □金融業 □資訊業 □軍警 □傳播業 □自由業

　　　□服務業 □公務員 □教職　□學生 □其他＿＿＿＿＿

(請沿線對摺寄回,謝謝!)

秀威與 BOD

BOD（Books On Demand）是數位出版的大趨勢，秀威資訊率先運用 POD 數位印刷設備來生產書籍，並提供作者全程數位出版服務，致使書籍產銷零庫存，知識傳承不絕版，目前已開闢以下書系：

一、BOD　學術著作—專業論述的閱讀延伸
二、BOD　個人著作—分享生命的心路歷程
三、BOD　旅遊著作—個人深度旅遊文學創作
四、BOD　大陸學者—大陸專業學者學術出版
五、POD　獨家經銷—數位產製的代發行書籍

BOD 秀威網路書店：www.showwe.com.tw
政府出版品網路書店：www.govbooks.com.tw

　　永不絕版的故事・自己寫・永不休止的音符・自己唱